INDECENT PRINCE CHARMING

Giselle Waters

www.BOROUGHSPUBLISHINGGROUP.com

ISBN: 978-1-953810-35-9

To my mom.

I'll never forget watching romance movies with her, eating popcorn, and talking about life, love, and cute guys. Mom would've loved I wrote a romance novel. She always supported me.

I love you mom. This one's for you.
RIP

ACKNOWLEDGMENTS

Thank you to the editors and staff at Boroughs Publishing Group for seeing something in me and my story enough to make a writer's dream come true.

I also want to thank anyone who takes the time to read this book.

INDECENT PRINCE CHARMING

Chapter One

Adrian rested his shoulder against a cool marble column on the second floor and watched the whole affair with amusement. He was a bit bored, but he sipped his wine and let the chatter surround him. The whole night seemed to be dragging with a déjà vu-like familiarity. He would add tonight to his collection of his life's less remarkable memories. At least the event was in San Francisco's City Hall.

He gave a quick nostalgic sniff to the city he loved. The decorated hall smelled of perfumed jasmine. Even dressed up for a charity ball, the hall couldn't hide its old white marble smell. He liked the way he felt standing next to the magnificent stone staircase and large open room. He heard the instrumentals echoing under the alabaster dome.

He looked over at the first floor with a passing glance of the crowd. He felt removed and suffered from *ennui*, impatient for the night to be over. He struggled to remember the name of the charity for which he was attending the gala. He looked up and to the right to the sign that read: *Esperanza*. He said the name quietly to himself as he recalled the charity built schools in underprivileged areas around the globe. It was always important to remember to whom he gave his money.

Adrian didn't have much endurance for parties like this. He could get more done with a phone and a computer than he could dancing. He preferred the seat behind his desk and the glow of his computer screen, not the forced politeness these diversions always required. However, every year he forced himself to attend to a few *good will* projects he'd collected, including the fundraisers. He had a short list of ten such charities he liked. Esperanza had seemed a worthy enough cause.

He donated one hundred fifty K per year to each organization, which was all good press. The allotments made his business and personal résumé seem generous, but in actuality it pinched his wallet no more than a cup of coffee. The donation allowed him to pretend his life had more meaning. The best part was he didn't have to get his hands dirty to do it. He'd leave it to the volunteers to soil their fingertips. All he had to do was to show up in one of his bespoke formal wear suits. He liked having an excuse to wear them.

Adrian hadn't bothered to bring a date. There wasn't a woman of his acquaintance who he'd wanted to bring, much less talk to. He had too many other pursuits more interesting than female companions. He preferred buying and selling properties, and enlarging his holdings and his various accounts and financial portfolios. In the past, occasionally, he'd diverted his attention to females now and then, but it was hard to turn his head for long.

His tastes extended to mostly blondes, and only rarely. Adrian's gaze wandered as he thought about getting home, throwing his jacket in the corner of his closet, and slipping into his silky sheets. He'd browse through emails filled with proposals as he gently lulled himself to sleep with figures, valuations, and equity jumping over fences.

His eyes focused when he saw a woman approach the precipice of the staircase and stop.

She wasn't his type. Adrian's entire recorded sexual history consisted of forgettable partners and quick hook-ups. Compared to this vision, the women he'd bedded had been girlish, slender, and completely garden variety. Standing in front of Adrian was a remarkable woman.

His brain screamed in recognition. Who was the unapologetically voluptuous goddess with eager curves and flowing black hair? Adrian was arrested by the sight of her. There was a charmingly mischievous smile playing about her full red lips, decadently wicked on her innocent looking face. Adrian could only imagine what those lips would feel like on him. He was struck with the urge to pull her into his arms and kiss her.

Her big brown eyes were looking everywhere but at him, so he took advantage and stared at her indulgently. There was a mysterious pause as she considered the crowd. Her careful gaze landed on each person with a calculated presence. She was running this show. He echoed her actions, but stared at her alone.

His nostrils flared at the heady recognition of desire as he looked at lines of her feminine figure. He felt his interest fan into fire as he studied her sinful form, the way the black silk threads of her gown cinched at the apex of her waist before flaring into fullness of her hips. She had the most generous cleavage, which the gown accentuated by dipping into a deep vee. The sleeves draped off the crests of her exposed shoulders.

Her dark hair spilled over her back and he could easily imagine what she might look like without that magnificent gown. She was a wanton angel, but looked untouchable. He wanted to see that celestial being completely undressed.

She was everything Adrian never knew he wanted a woman to look like, and he couldn't help but watch.

Unable to turn away, he watched as the goddess in black swanned gently down each step. Time had stopped. He watched the slow waves of her dark hair slip over her shoulder as her face disappeared from view. He admired her movement as she descended the stairs, and the way her dress moved as she walked. Adrian was mesmerized by the expanse of caramel skin as her thigh slashed through the dress's deep slit with each step she took.

These rampant flames of desire were startling and completely unsettling. He didn't have time for this rabbit hole of distraction.

As he lost sight of her, he found himself wandering to the steps powerless as his feet drove him to the top of the staircase where he looked for her again.

***

Hana stood on the top of the stairs looking over the gala with pride. Spring in San Francisco meant it was a bit chilly even indoors, but the glittering rows of yellow-white bulbs dangling overhead and the musicians seated on the stage on the ground floor where the sounds of a cello and violins floated over the fragrant floral scented air made everything magical.

Her charity, Esperanza, was on display tonight. Hundreds of people dressed like royals and dignitaries were here to support her cause. The marbled city hall was decorated like a wedding, and people stood in line to have their photos professionally taken.

Flowers floated to the ceiling in heavy crystal vases on tall cocktail tables, and wine flowed through the crowd.

The gowns were long, and the formal wear was sharp. It was the type of charity gala that not only increased tax write-offs, but also looked good for promotion. She hoped that would be enough for some people. Others she hoped to convince with her speech, the speeches of supporters, and a gentle but generous plying of wine. She wanted people to donate with their money and not with their words.

Hana had to settle the nerves in her stomach with a deep breath. She calmed herself with a reassuring set of her shoulders and began walking down the stairs. The whole room was watching. She had never taken this long to get ready in her life, but felt as confident as she could in her expensive gown. She'd dressed formally and was unused to the way the black silk gown hugged the skin off her shoulders and split generously up to her thigh.

There was barely enough inky black fabric covering the shapes of her breasts to be decent, but the dress was elegantly adult in a way that accentuated Hana's curves. She'd never felt sexier. Her curls were coming off her head in delicate waves down the right side of her neck. She let her tall black heels do the talking as she slowly descended the steps. She felt like there were a hundred of them.

She kept her head held high as she looked for a familiar face to ease herself and saw Bianca. The tall woman with cherry red hair stood out in the crowd even though she also was wearing a black dress. Bianca and Hana's other friend Taron, as well as some members of Esperanza's staff, were standing in a group nearby. Taron and Bianca greeted Hana as she neared. They looked as excited as she was.

Hana told Taron as they hugged, "You look so beautiful, *mi amor*."

Taron was her oldest friend and Hana was proud to stand next to her co-creator of their nonprofit. Taron looked gorgeous under the warm yellow lights of the grand hall. Her platinum blonde curls coiled sharply on top of her head looking brighter than usual, and her skin looked more golden.

She was wearing a tailored black suit that accentuated her femininity with crystal embossed lapels buttoned at her cinched waist. She looked powerful and uncompromisingly female. Hana marveled at the way her best friend had transformed.

"You too, mama." Taron stated. "You look stunning in that dress."

Taron's hug was reassuring and needed at that moment. She and Taron were Cinderellas at their own ball waiting for San Francisco's elite to get down on a bent knee and write them lots and lots of checks.

Hana loved the way she felt and how beautiful the gala turned out. City Hall was decorated like it was her wedding, and she was wearing her dream black wedding gown. Her partner in crime was right there with her.

"We are going to raise some money tonight," Taron said.

Hana moved to greet Bianca, accepting a hug from the slight woman. Her college friend was wearing lacy confection for the evening, and Hana was glad to see her familiar face. The CFO was sharp, savvy, and made an excellent addition to the Esperanza team. They all believed in the charity and what it stood for: building schools where children needed them the most.

Hana wanted her friends to have fun tonight, but she didn't want to be distracted from the reason they were here. To get people to donate money. Money she could use for every tool needed to build another school, and every pencil she wanted to put in a child's hand. She hoped they could raise enough to make this whole glitzy event worth it.

As Taron handed her a glass of white wine, and Hana said, "I hope people put their money where their mouths are. People talk a lot but don't donate."

Bianca stared wide-eyed. "I think this is the closest I've ever been to so many really wealthy people."

Hana rolled her eyes. "I need them to write checks, not stand around drinking our wine."

Taron snorted. All these years, her best friend had never wavered in her faith in Esperanza. Taron put her hands on her hips. She'd been determined from day one to make Esperanza a success. Hana knew that this charity would be nothing without Taron. Year after year, she relied on her best friend to keep her calm, grounded.

Taron said, "Worse comes to worst, we can go back to my mom's garage. She'd give us the family discount again."

Hana laughed, but it was mixed with genuine relief that they'd made it out of the "family garage." Hana still had the hunger pains from all the late nights and payless days that came from starting their own non-profit. They had been door-to-door salespeople working out of Taron's mom's garage. They built schools from the sweat of their own brows. Hana had personally helped build fifteen schools and hoped tonight would raise enough to build five more.

"I'm nervous about my speech," Hana said while looking around.

She worried her shaking hands would carry to her voice. Nothing gave off uneasy like a gentle wobble in her speech. She took another breath to calm herself. She reminded herself why she was here.

Taron took Hana's wine glass from her. "Mind moves matter," she reminded Hana.

Hana and Taron both remembered their schoolgirl Latin days like they were yesterday. The old Virgil quote which had evolved to mean mind over matter. It had become a saying they used to tell each other to buck up, put on armor and a shield against the world. It was code between friends that it was time to put on a show.

Taron and she shared a bond from spending their entire lives together. But tonight, she alone needed to get her ass on the stage. Hana nodded and walked over to the edge of the stage. She took a microphone and a fresh glass of wine from a circulating host. Her steps climbing the stairs were slow and deliberate. *Mind moves matter* she repeated to herself. *I can do this.*

Hana squared her shoulders and held her head high as she raised her glass to the ceiling and began a toast. Hana tried to meet every eye as she introduced herself as the CEO of Esperanza to a hundred guests.

She wanted to say to the crowd: *Here's to you. Give me your money.* Instead she settled on: "Thank you everyone for attending. Here's to you and every student we put in a classroom."

Everyone clapped, and she took a deep sip of her wine. Glasses tipped into the air and followed her lead.

***

Adrian didn't take a drink. He was standing in the alcove watching the charity executive speak. He had a glass in his hand when she made her toast, but he wouldn't have turned his attention away from her even for a split second.

Hana Romero. He finally had a name for the intriguing heart-shaped face. He was impressed. He could tell she was a younger woman. He guessed her to be in her late twenties, but she had clearly accomplished many things in her short lifetime. He had never built any schools, or any building for that matter, in whatever country she was talking about right now. Adrian was certainly happy to lend his annual stipend for such an interesting charity. She was a unique species, this Ms. Romero.

He realized the lust he was feeling for her also was tied with an irritating urge to get close to her. She was fascinating. She had a way about the cadence of her speech, and an intensity in her eyes that made him want to hear her, even if he wasn't personally invested in what she was saying. She finished speaking, and another woman went on stage in an eye-catching jeweled suit and picked up where Hana left off.

As his dream woman left the stage, he wondered if he'd get the chance to talk to her. He waited through three more speakers. When the last finished, he saw the co-founders of the charity mingling through the crowd. He heard the band begin to play again. Naturally, people moved away from the dancers forming in the middle of the room.

Adrian saw his opportunity and walked over to the enchanting Ms. Romero, standing face to face with his fascination at last.

Chapter Two

Hana stopped hearing the music as she saw the tall and intimidating figure approach her. She had to admit he was startlingly handsome, and she could tell by the cut of his suit that he was filthy rich. The confident stranger walked toward her with a purpose. She compared his gait to a shark in the water. She could feel it in the way her heartbeat ramped up a little as he neared, and she studied the predatory gleam in his green eyes.

His attention was undivided as he came straight at her. Hana tried to decipher him. It looked like that suit was made to measure; his lean muscular frame was topped by a model's face. His short blond hair was combed elegantly to the side, highlighting his patrician good looks. The package was fantastic, yet Hana couldn't help but stare at his lips. She noticed them immediately. The impossibly sensual curve that made his expression fearsome as he stared at her.

He wasn't scowling, but his lips weren't shaped into anything approaching a smile. He looked to be in his early thirties, but he had a cynical air about him. With that razor-sharp jawline and chiseled cheekbones, he looked positively dangerous.

When he walked up to her, she expected him to bow. His green gaze was intense, and he didn't immediately speak. She felt like he was assessing her.

"Adrian Douglas," he said after an interminable pause, and held out his hand.

She realized he was offering it for her to shake it. He was so formal she couldn't help but laugh a little. "Hana Romero," she returned and shook his warm, large hand.

She was pulling hers away as he turned his palm up. He offered it to her, and she had the urge to immediately return her hand to his. She realized he was asking her to dance.

"Would you care to dance?" He confirmed her suspicion.

She stared wordlessly into his eyes. She didn't come to dance, but she found it hard to say no to this man. She asked herself why she should deprive herself of the pleasure of being in close proximity to such a good-looking specimen of the male species. He was complimenting her with a dance. It could be fun, she reassured herself.

Hana promised herself this one dance.

She nodded and smiled, taking his hand as he led her to the dance floor. He pulled her into a partner's embrace. His hands making him familiar with the shape of her waist while his fingers splayed to rest on her backside. His large hand on her body felt better than it should have.

Hana became intimately close with her tall stranger as he led her into a slow dance. He took her other hand in his, and it felt small in his grasp. The music softly played as he turned them to the rhythm. Hana's feet swept along the marble floor as he held her close making her more aware his nearness while they danced. She could smell some curated scent of man and expensive fragrance. He was all muscle under that suit. She could feel it under her fingers. His hard toned body felt amazing as she put her hand on his firm shoulder.

"Thank you for coming and hopefully donating to Esperanza," she said to distract her or else she'd have no choice but to examine this pleasurable sense of intimacy. "We hope you're enjoying your evening," she said graciously.

He twirled her effortlessly in response, and she could see he was enjoying this waltz with her. Hana laughed and gloried in the dance. She was swept up in the moment. The wine was pleasant, and the man was handsome, so she let herself enjoy it.

She wanted to savor the feeling of a man holding her. It had been a long time since she was in anyone's arms. This stranger's touch felt right, and his hand on her back made her feel protected. She had to admit it was nice to let her guard down, but knew she didn't have time for dates, pretty boys, or things that required emotional upkeep.

Adrian Douglas, he'd said. She met his stare again. Mr. Douglas was intimidating. He looked like trouble, but he danced like a dream. Hana didn't expect to ever see him again after tonight, but he was certainly memorable.

His emerald eyes were innocently blank, but she could see he had a dark edge behind the façade. She knew enough about men to be wary of such intensity.

"The hall is charmingly done," he commented politely.

She decided it didn't hurt to be honest with him and smiled with as much sweetness as she could muster. "Thanks," she said. "I never imagined I would be dancing under the dome, drinking wine, and asking people to help me build schools."

He laughed softly, and she was struck by how truly devastating he was when he smiled. He made her stomach flip as he looked at her. This was where the wolf was evident in an elegant sheep thread suit. His eyes were practically devilish as they slipped to curious investigation of her gown.

She flushed under his scrutiny. It felt unsettling to have his gaze on her especially when it spoke of intention and what he could do to her if he caught her alone. Hana realized that he was sexy enough to make her curious, and that kind of power was dangerous.

***

Adrian was trying something he never did: he was trying to get to know her. He usually skipped the formalities and got straight down to business. She was challenging, but he liked the feeling of her in his arms, and the way her body felt under his fingers. He was satiated by the awareness of her sensual waistline and hips under his hand. He tightened his grip on her gently.

The truth was he hadn't seen or been near a woman like this in a long time. She was sexy in a slow burn kind of way, and it made his blood boil and his urges turn animal. He wanted this woman in a way he had never desired a woman. He wanted her in his bed. But he was wary of his urgent desire for her, so as they turned around the room, Adrian tried to dampen his ardor.

To no avail.

She kept smiling up at him with those plump crimson lips and he found himself tempted beyond anything he'd ever known. He'd never been shy to ask for what he wanted, and he faced the inevitability that it was only a matter of time until he tried to kiss her.

Hana looked up at him and moved her hand from his shoulder to the back of his neck. Adrian gasped from her nearness. Being next to the electrifying Ms. Romero was startling.

"I was hoping you might be interested in letting me take you out to dinner," he stated.

***

Hana smiled. She was flattered by the offer. She was going to reject him, of course, but the confirmation of his admiration was gratifying. This man was as stunning as he was wealthy. She knew her mother would have approved of this one for sure, but Hana didn't.

Money was inconsequential to her personally, and everything to her when it came to Esperanza. She knew a healthy bank account mattered to other women, but Hana didn't care. Maybe it was because she was practically married to Esperanza, or the fact that she barely had time to date. Regardless, she wasn't going to give him a chance. She didn't have time for rich boys and the effort that a man like this would take.

She could tell a man like Adrian needed a certain kind of attention. He had a smoldering intensity in his eyes that made her question what he would be like in the bedroom. He didn't seem like the courtship and wait kind of man. She could already tell Adrian Douglas didn't make long conversation. He stated what he wanted and went about getting it.

He wasn't going to have her.

She laughed him off. "We're not compatible, Adrian. I remain optimistic though that you'll still donate even if I don't go to dinner with you," she said enjoying the light tease made to a man who looked like he didn't laugh much.

"I will," he said levelly, and seemed to absorb the refusal easily. "Although I wonder why you say we're incompatible. Everyone has to eat at some time in the day. I'm sure we could manage."

She shook her head with mirth. He was clueless and charming, though arrogant. He was a little too forward, and way too handsy. Then again, Hana didn't ask him to move his hands. She like the feeling too much.

They kept dancing, and she finalized her opinion about him. He clearly had presumptions about her. He had assumed she'd say yes immediately. He had the looks and money that surely meant not a lot of people refused him.

"It's not the time that's the issue, Mr. Douglas," she said, clarifying her refusal. "It's you and me." She poked him because it was too easy, and he probably never had anyone turn him down. She continued, "Your cufflinks are the price of my car, and I've made a career of building schools with my own two hands. It would never work." She gave him a saucy smile. "What do you do for a living, if anything at all?"

He cocked his head as if he disagreed, but not about the price of his cufflinks. She was joking with him, but suddenly felt guilty for yanking his chain. Hana was criticizing him for being rich, and he was exactly the type of person she needed to donate to her cause.

She wasn't the best at public relations, and time and time again her mouth got her in trouble. Her mother had always warned her to think twice before she spoke, but all the good advice went out the window when she was talking to this handsome stranger. She didn't want to leave their conversation on a bad note, so she gave him another winning smile. A *please don't tell everyone the CEO is crazy* kind of smile.

He answered her question as they continued their turn around the room. "I acquire corporations."

Oh, no. A raider. She couldn't poke fun at that.

Now he sounded like an insensitive rich guy who had no clue that real people worked for these corporations he bought and sold. He sounded like a kid with a magnifying glass, callous and unaware. She realized he was the last kind of man she could ever get involved with and was glad to have refused him.

"Corporations are made up of people. Are you saying you acquire people?" she asked dryly.

"I agree, they are," he said, his bright green eyes staring unapologetically into hers. His voice became ceremonious again and distant. She was startled by his directness, and his tone was ice cold. He continued, "However, I can see you are determined to misunderstand me. Next time I can wear a less formal suit if you like, but it was only an invitation to dinner. If I knew I was in a job interview I would have sold myself better."

She smarted from his reply. He had a cleverness with words and a sharp wit. He was smiling again, but she could tell it was a disingenuous. He was throwing her off balance.

Adrian was clearly displeased and there was an indescribable gleam in his eyes. He was too dangerous for dinner, that was certain. She had to shut this down completely.

The song was ending, and they stopped in place, still face to face with him looking at her intently. She looked up at him and met his gaze levelly. "I had the pleasure laughing with you Mr. Douglas. I anticipate I won't ever forget meeting you." She was sure of it.

He nodded. She still had her hand on his, and he brought it up to brush those luscious lips whisper light over the sensitive skin of her knuckles, sending small jolts of electricity up her arm.

Adrian seemed like James Bond. Cool, calm, and collected while he made her feel like they were the only two people in the room. He radiated intensity and bad intentions.

"I *anticipate* when we meet again." He punctuated the word as he kissed her hand and the gentlemanly gesture topped off the happily ever after evening she had been having for a few brief minutes.

He was a bit more anti-hero than white knight, but this time he did bow before he walked away.

She watched him as he left.

Chapter Three

Three days after receiving more donations than Esperanza ever received before, Hana knew the ball was over, and the magic was gone. Her fairy tale charity felt had turned into a cautionary tale of trust gone wrong. This morning she'd learned Bianca embezzled all of their fundraising efforts, which meant they couldn't build more schools.

It meant no more pencils for her to give out, and the complete end to Esperanza. Hana would've given anything in the world to not be watching what she was seeing on TV. Her charity's name flashed on the screen as news stations reported the theft. She realized she was crying when the tears fell on the remote. Today felt like she was watching a high-speed crash of a bullet train to Kyoto, everything was happening so fast and so slow at the same time.

She spent the next five hours scrolling on her phone through the articles about what Bianca had done. It was all over the internet. The ten million they'd raised over the course of three years, gone in an instant. Bianca was nowhere to be found, and Hana was falling apart. She lay sobbing on the floor and struggled to breathe.

The betrayal cut her to the core. She'd met with Taron to confirm her worst nightmare and learned it was real life. She hadn't believed it 'til she saw Taron's face. Bianca was gone, and so was any hope of Esperanza remaining viable.

Hana found herself screaming at the TV as she sat alone watching the news. Her charity was finally in the media's eye, but for all the wrong reasons. All of her contributors' money had been stolen by a woman Hana had trusted as a dear and close friend and colleague.

She felt sick. In her mind she saw all of the schools disappearing from the world. She thought of the woman who had betrayed her with heartbreak and anger.

Most of all, Hana was angry at herself for being so blind.

Bianca hadn't merely skimmed some money off the top, she'd stolen their entire cache. Some of the money had been meant to cover expenses Esperanza was going to incur, and bills it had already accumulated. They wouldn't be able to stay afloat. Esperanza owed too many people money.

Hana needed to pay Esperanza's rent and her own. She'd already paid a lot of contractors in anticipation of building schools. The entire staff had been counting on that money.

Bianca's heartless face flashed on the screen and Hana studied the unreadable brown eyes. She didn't know that woman at all, though she could recall every conversation they'd ever had.

The terrible loop of realization replayed in her mind. Even up until the gala, Bianca had pledged to be in love with the company's mission. She hadn't indicated any personal financial distress. If she'd needed money, Hana would have helped her.

But this wasn't about Bianca being strapped. She was a thief who'd seen an easy mark and played being Hana's friend for three years, worming her way into Esperanza so she could take the money and run.

Esperanza had been a success up until now. To date, they'd built thirty schools around the world. They'd never be able to build another school again. She was going to have to shut down her operation. Her donors had trusted her to do something good with their contributions. She had failed them and every child she thought she was going to turn into a student.

For weeks after learning of Bianca's duplicity, Hana found herself waking up and getting ready to go to the office reflexively. Every morning she laid out her clothes for work only to realize there was no charity to go to. The minute the theft had been discovered, Hana had hired a team of financial forensic investigators to work out of Esperanza's headquarters, but their work had been thwarted by the NYPD, who'd taken every computer and file in the office. Now that the equipment was returned, she'd have to go to the office to pick up the mail.

Finally, compelled by the desire to be in the place she'd loved, she walked into her office building feeling like she was preparing Esperanza for its funeral. As she made her way into the Esperanza's space, she tried not to look at Bianca's desk and all the hateful things Hana wanted to think about her former friend.

Hana regretted the day she had invited that woman to join Esperanza. Her hiring mistake had been a rookie move. She hadn't vetted Bianca. She'd trusted her because she was a friend. Now, the money was gone and so was Bianca.

The police had left the office in shambles. Sheets of paper hung off desks and piles of paperwork were left in the middle of the floor. Most of the desktop computers had been returned, except for Bianca's.

It looked like a war zone.

She hadn't yet responded to her staff's suspicions that Esperanza was finished. They would have to find new jobs. The least she could do was write them recommendations strong enough to land them new positions. Lord knew she would never be able to pay her employees again.

Hana walked to her office with heavy steps and sat down at her desk feeling like she had lived a different life compared to the last time she'd sat there. She rifled through collected invoices and various communications, finding herself shaken to her core. She wondered if life would ever be okay again. She was feeling hopeless as she sifted through the papers wondering how she'd been so blind.

Ten million dollars gone.

After going through bills she wouldn't be able to pay, cancelled work orders, and some letters from donors expressing their sorrow over the loss of a worthy charity, Hana lifted a thick envelope with Douglas Holdings embossed across the center. Adrian Douglas's company.

She ripped open the envelope to find a letter inside that stated Douglas Holdings was willing to pledge a million dollars to Hana Romero, which she presumed was to help get Esperanza back on its feet. But first, the letter directed, she'd have to meet with the corporate officers. The letter made no mention of Bianca's theft, only the offer of one million dollars. She picked up the shredded envelope and held the top together. The letter was written after the scandal hit the media. After the police had finished their investigation.

The money was generous, more generous than she could have ever anticipated. It didn't say it was from Adrian, but everything about the letter sounded like the man she'd danced with at a ball that seemed to have been a dream. Vague and short, the letter was puzzling.

She put it down, and guessed like its likely author—Adrian was a man of few words—the money would be enough of an inducement to get her to Douglas Holdings.

She replayed their dance the night of the gala. Sure, it'd been wonderful, but it hadn't been a million-dollar dance. Well, not for her.

She'd laughed when she rejected him, but Adrian hadn't found her refusal funny. He turned away in a pique. That night had been sultry and magical, and she couldn't deny the zinging connection between them, but it hadn't progressed beyond that intimate dance.

Hana decided to call the company phone number at the top of the letter. She read the letter again as the phone was ringing. It struck her as beyond odd the letter was so vague.

Please schedule a meeting at your earliest convenience to discuss. Hana wondered what there was to discuss if he truly meant to give Esperanza what he offered. She scoffed at the word *meeting* in particular, especially since he hadn't mentioned his own name in the letter. She didn't want to meet him, but she couldn't expect he'd wire money to Esperanza without having some personal assurances as how Hana would handle the donation. After everything that'd happened, he was owed at least that. She was transferred from one person to another before finally she was connected to the man who handled Mr. Douglas's personal schedule.

"Ah, Ms. Romero," the young, cultured, slightly British sounding voice began. "Mr. Douglas has been anticipating your reply. Currently, he's on another call, but has asked me to open his calendar to your meeting time preference."

She listened and shook her head. How strange. It was as if Adrian was trying to make himself seem more mysterious and aloof. If he wanted to see her so badly, why didn't he include his personal cell number so she could reach him directly?

"Ms. Romero," the assistant called. She'd been wool gathering. "When would you like to schedule a meeting with Mr. Douglas?"

"Today, anytime," she said quickly.

They agreed to three this afternoon. When Hana hung up she felt a little sullied. Sure, Adrian was good looking, but he was a typical superficial rich boy with flirty hands. She hoped he didn't repeat his offer of a date to her. God, meeting with him couldn't be about that, could it?

To clear her mind, she decided to have a light lunch and walk to his office afterward. She was a little terrified as she made her way downtown to his high-rise building, a glass and chrome monolith as inviting as cold steel.

As she went up the elevator, she caught herself readjusting her dress, and she never fidgeted with her clothes. She hadn't thought to apply any makeup or wear a suit. She liked her army green empire dress, but she found herself feeling underdressed for what she presumed were the stuffy offices of Douglas Holdings. Though, the dress accentuated the deep curve of her waist and showed a fair amount of cleavage, she thought it looked tasteful.

She promised herself she'd ignore any attraction she might feel for Adrian. He was a cad, and she'd do well to remember that.

She arrived at the floor of Douglas Holdings' offices and his assistant came to the reception area – the outer offices weren't stuffy, but were stark with black chairs, white walls and a white marble floor - nodded at her name and asked her to wait while he paged Adrian. She was handed a bone-white, thick and weighty business card and turned it over in her hand. She felt the embossed engraving with Adrian's name on it.

She almost laughed. How ridiculous to be in this formal atmosphere after everything that had happened.

When the young man led her into Adrian's office, she straightened her shoulders and put on her game face.

Chapter Four

Adrian looked up and saw Hana entering his office. God, she was beautiful. He wanted to gather her in his arms and hold her close. Instead, he pulled himself together and stood to greet her. He had to push away the guilt that danced at the edges of his mind for the guise he'd used to get her here. The ends would justify the means, he told himself.

As he got closer, he saw she'd been crying and looked drawn. Given everything that had happened, feeling betrayed and discouraged was to be expected. He didn't understand sympathy, and didn't see its usefulness. The best way to acquire something was to point out how much of a need he was fulfilling. Hana needed his help and he was going to use her situation to press his suit. Yes, not necessarily seemly, but he had an opening and he was going to take it.

Contrary to her sad expression, she was wearing a playfully feminine green dress that suited her shape. Her dark hair was free of artifice and was wildly curled around her face. She looked younger in the daylight, which he found even more appealing than the stunning woman he'd danced with at the gala. His body hummed at their current proximity, as if it recognized what it most desired. All of the promise of his memories of her were hardly enough compared to the real thing.

He had been obsessed with seeing her again and had made a promise to himself that he would. He didn't have anything to do with the circumstances that gave him this edge, and he wouldn't have wanted that for her, but he saw no reason not to capitalize on the situation. He didn't care if what he was doing was wrong. She was here, and he would do what he had to. He wasn't going to let her walk away this time.

Adrian had never gone to these lengths to be with a woman. He hadn't needed to, or hadn't been inclined. But Hana was special.

Something he had to have. Using Hana's need for donations to keep Esperanza afloat and offering a million dollars was a small price to pay to play out this temptation. If he could bed her, he'd finally forget her and get back to doing what he did best: making money.

Adrian wanted to get this fascination out of his system. Hana was starting to get under his skin. He would never admit how many nights in the past few weeks he had replayed their dance in his head. He repeated every word and debated about what he could have said differently. Then he realized he could solve the problem easily with the way he always solved financial roadblocks.

Throw money at the problem.

It wasn't his fault she'd hired a thief, but he was going to take advantage of the situation. He was going to point out how many holes there were in the ship of her charity. She was going to sink. Without his money, Esperanza would be gone.

Adrian's plan was ruthless and exploited his leverage. He was going to use every tactic he knew to convince her to agree to his offer.

He started with business because that's the only way he knew. Adrian didn't do small talk. He gestured to an empty chair then backed up to sit on his side of the desk. She sat down quietly, and he followed suit. Adrian held his empty hand out over the surface of his desk, palm up.

"May I?" he asked innocently.

He was indicating in the direction of the business card in her hand. She gave it up to him, eyeing him as she pushed it on the desk. He took the card and wrote on it in his meticulously trained scrawl.

"This is my personal number," he said. He picked up the card and reached over the desk to put it in front of her. He set his pen to the side and looked up at her. The silence between them intensified the moment.

Hana took the card and nodded silently. He looked her in the eyes. He knew there was a chance she'd sue him or worse. He took the risk. "I'm about to make you an offer you won't be able to decide on until you've had time to think about it." He knew after their dance, when she walked away from him, he still wanted her even though she'd refused him. He found himself thinking about her long after he had left that night. Then he saw her charity implode, he knew he'd found his chance

"Offer?" She cocked her head curiously. "I thought you were making a donation."

He shook his head. "I don't make donations in the million-dollar range." Intentionally, he'd been vague. Now it was time to reveal what he intended. A small part of him acknowledged that he was a bad man. He didn't care. He accepted he was doing what he had to, what he needed to do to have her.

If the worst thing he ever did was having Hana, he'd be happy with his sins.

She was fingering the card in her hand, and he found himself distracted as he watched. He tried not to dwell on the guilt. She seemed so innocent, so vulnerable and alone in his lair. But Adrian wanted her in his bed and he didn't care about the moral toll.

She looked up and said, "I don't understand."

***

Hana watched his handsome expressionless face looking for clue as to what he meant. She didn't understand what he was saying. He was going to give her a million dollars in some sort of exchange. An offer she would have to think about. She looked out the floor to ceiling glass wall behind him, dazed by this odd and unsettling turn of events.

His office was a huge room, sparsely furnished, with his magnificent mahogany desk placed dead center in front of the wall of window. He had an impressive view of the San Francisco skyline. Men like him didn't deserve such a beautiful vista.

She felt like she was being asked to agree to a Faustian dinner with the devil. But as devilish as he was, he was ice cold. He sat there silently gazing at her, his green eyes trained on hers, aloof and removed in his obviously handmade suit.

That pouty mouth of his never smiled and those chiseled cheekbones were painfully aristocratic. She was reminded of how it felt when his attention was on her. When his hands were on her. She tried to focus and make him talk sense.

"Tell me what the offer is," she demanded quietly.

"I'll pledge my money, but you have to sleep with me," he stated as if the bargain was a typical business transaction. As if it weren't clear enough, she saw those incredible lips form another word as her ears burned with understanding. "Sex," he said firmly.

It was like a bucket of ice was thrown over her head. She had been shocked the day she found out about Bianca, but she was disgusted and appalled as she listened to his proposal. This is how he expected her to earn a million dollars.

She rose and set his card down on the desk. "I don't sell sex," she hissed. "I don't know what impression you got, but—"

"I didn't get that impression," he said calmly.

She was seething as she watched him talk. Lucifer in a tailored suit. He tried to make her his Lilith.

"I tried the old-fashioned way, now I'm trying the leverage way," he said coldly.

She couldn't believe what he was saying.

"That's disgusting," she called out between clenched teeth. He was really that privileged, he thought he could to buy her, as if any woman could be bought. Well, some could, but she didn't sell sex for a living. Sex meant something to her. It was a declaration of love she gave to the two lovers she'd cared about. She had only been with two boyfriends in her lifetime. She was inexperienced when it came to love, and even more so when it came to casual sex and the men who asked for it.

She had never hated a man more than she hated Adrian right now.

"Is it?" He smirked. "It doesn't have to be. We could have fun. You have something I want, and I have something you want." He shrugged as if his offer weren't the most horrible thing a person had ever said to her.

"This is insulting," she half yelled. She didn't care if that personal assistant or the entire floor heard her. "You're awful for trying to take advantage of me."

"Yes," he agreed without any hint of remorse as he put his hands together into a pyramid under his chin. "I want you, and I'll pay for it if I have to. I'd pay more if you asked." He tilted his head. "I know you've never done this before."

He made it sound like he was talking about buying a company. No, a service, like she was making his coffee not pricing how much it would cost to bed her. He had valued her expensively and hoped the high price would flatter her. She realized this man was lecherous, vile, and everything her mother had warned her about, but nowhere near enough to absorb this.

She shook her head. She pitied him that he needed to buy women as a means to manufacture relationships.

"I don't want your money," she insisted fiercely.

"But you do. You've taken it before to build schools," he said and pushed back his chair.

He was tall, at least six foot five, and she watched as he stretched the powerful muscles of his body and stood. He was commanding in appearance, and the embodiment of indecency and corrupt power.

"Now you can build a lot of them."

She tried to change tack. She wanted to point out how sympathetic her cause was. She could think of plenty of reasons why her charity was worthy of his donation. She would recite her entire speech if she had to. "Won't you give me the money because it's essential for Esperanza to continue its work?" His expression hardened. He wasn't giving an inch. He wasn't offering her money because he believed in Esperanza.

Adrian smoothed down his suit jacket. He started from behind his desk. It was unwise to stay in the wolf's den. She knew she should leave.

"Not when I can have you. You are…" She felt the flush of embarrassment creep up her neck. That a man would make her such an offer and not value her for anything other than her body... she fought the surge of emotions and realized, he should feel shame not her. She didn't back down as he came to stand before her, but was silent as he talked.

"...I don't have words for what you are." Adrian said softly. "I would treat you like the beautiful and special woman you are. Just because I'm trying to buy you, doesn't mean I don't recognize your value."

"Ten million for a year," he said calmly, throwing out the number like it was nothing more than a game.

Hana was going to be sick. She knew what she could do with ten million dollars. She could build so many schools, help so many children with that kind of money. A man like him didn't blink at such a figure while it would take her years to raise that amount in donations.

The number stuck in her gut because it was the exact amount Bianca had stolen from Esperanza. She hated he knew that and used it to his benefit. He knew she was desperate, and he scavenged from the roadkill of her charity. She knew he wanted her, but she couldn't believe a man would want her like that.

She hated him for his proposition, for thinking she would ever do it, and for asking her in the first place. She started to turn from him, and he didn't stop her.

"I don't think we'd want each other that long," he said callously. He probably thought he sounded like a gentleman. "But I'd pay for the privilege of your time."

Hana held up her hand to stop him from speaking. She'd had enough. "I can't listen to any more of this."

Arrogant to the cores, he continued, ignoring her wishes. "With the stipulation that three million of it be a personal salary."

He refused to respect her. Thinking that dangling that carrot would make what he was offering palatable. He was insufferable. She wanted to slap him. She pictured herself getting carried outside the building resisting the security as they attempted to make her leave.

She hissed, "A salary for sleeping with you."

He nodded and his eyes were so dark. He didn't smile, he merely arranged his tie and leaned back against his desk.

"Anytime I want you," he declared insolently.

She screamed, "Adrian. Enough."

His name reverberated through the room. Hana knew he was the worst kind of man, but even now he had her heart beating. She didn't like how the lecherous proposal did something strange to her senses, and against her will she became more aware of him. His intimidating male presence that threatened her to crave what a strong man like that could provide. He was telling her it didn't have to be unpleasant, and Hana knew deep inside that he might be right. Still she couldn't stand his audacity, and his lack of decency.

***

Adrian had never seen her so animated. Her chest heaved with emotion and he knew he had crossed a line. He stopped talking and watched her. His beautiful martyr.

He'd stake ten million dollars that she would sacrifice herself for her schools. He knew the minute he'd heard her challenge she'd do anything to keep Esperanza alive. Adrian knew people. Hana was selfless to her core.

That and her uncompromising center were what made her special, what made her irresistible. There was a hidden value to her, something that increased her worth tenfold. Adrian ignored his conscience.

His family would be disgusted with what he had proposed. They would have said that all the money he had made over the years had corrupted him. They'd be right. But still, he wanted this woman, and he meant to have her.

His proposal sat between them. Their relationship would forever be *after* the moment he tried to buy her.

She turned away from him again and walked wordlessly toward the door. He met her in three long strides and tried to hand her the business card, saying her name softly. "Hana."

She took the card from him and crumpled it in her fist, meeting his gaze. "I hope I never see you again, Mr. Douglas."

He nodded, opened the door, and watched her leave. He stared at her straight back, the way she walked, and the fierce determination of her anger.

He still wanted her.

He remembered the gala, and the feeling of her in his hands.

He'd have her any way he could get her.

Chapter Five

Hana went home and without success tried to erase the sordid encounter from her mind. She regretted ever meeting Adrian Douglas. As she closed the door to her apartment, she felt the fury rolling off of her in a heat-filled temper. She was angry the offer was made, and now, try as she may, it would be embedded in her brain forever.

She kicked off her shoes by the door, then walked into the living room/kitchen. Her humble open concept apartment was the size of her office, but she was proud she had no roommate. She could barely afford the walk-up and decorated it with refurbished finds she'd spent hours renovating, including her caution cone orange couch. It wasn't glamorous, but she'd been happy here while running her charity from startup to gala.

After they'd gotten Esperanza off the ground, it had taken them years to take in enough money to quit their "day" jobs and work there full time with salaries. Hana considered her home to be cluttered with life. She had little souvenirs and gifts from her travels, and as she looked at all the different trinkets and books, she was reminded of the times spent collecting them. She was happy to admit she'd built a school in every one of those places.

Hana wished she kept her apartment neater, but her life spilled out messily and unkept where it could. Her cat had turned out to be a destructive interior decorator. She was always finding him playing with the tassels of her couch's quilt and little things he had pulled from the counter to the floor.

At the first school she'd ever built in Laos, she'd acquired so many specially printed scarves that she'd decorated the walls with them. She had a heavy heart as she realized she'd never do that again. Then she turned to the dangling beads from Ghana, which hung from every lamp or hook in the room. Pumpkin played with those too.

She had a hard time looking at her place. She wondered if she'd even be able to afford it anymore. She'd have to get another job, or look for other sponsors. She hated how she immediately thought about what she could do with ten million dollars.

Then what she'd have to do to get that ten million dollars. She wasn't a virgin, and the night of the gala she'd admitted Adrian was handsome. But he wasn't Prince Charming, and his offer was an abomination. But, then again, she thought about how many schools she could build with ten million dollars.

Hana's thoughts turned to Bianca. The traitorous insider who stole every donation Hana and Taron managed to fundraise. Hana thought about what type of person Bianca was to have stolen that money when she knew what their charity was going to do with it. The money would build schools, pay all the employees and rent, and pay their debts to all the contractors who had bought the materials to start work on the first schools slotted for development.

There was a certain cruel irony in trusting Bianca as Esperanza's treasurer, especially when the next money Hana found herself being offered was Adrian Douglas propositioning her to be his private prostitute for ten million dollars.

He'd grow tired of her. That despicable thought played through her mind. He would have sex with her then leave her before a week. Men like that wanted only casual sex. It would probably be the most expensive one-night stand in history.

Something about it seemed simple when she phrased it that way. She wanted to call her mother and laugh about the crazy experience. But when she shut her eyes all she could see was Esperanza dying along with all Hana's hopes and dreams crashing into flames unless she succumbed to the cold allure of ten million dollars. Those cold green eyes and calm, steady voice that never wavered when Adrian offered to fund Esperanza via sex with Hana. Her heart was like lead as she thought about saying yes.

To accept his proposal went against every moral principle she had. Hana had a good head on her shoulders and she knew what he was offering was wrong. She'd always wanted love and affection, and an easy relationship filled with humor and friendship. Adrian's proposal skipped any notion of romance. Hana's feelings didn't factor into the equation.

Now that chivalry was dead, men like him could make offers that women like her had to consider. She'd never wanted gifts from boyfriends, much less exchange love for money. Her mother always taught her to be independent and never count on a man for anything. Now she had to choose between saying yes to a man she didn't like, never mind care for, and the charity she had loved from day one.

She told herself sex was nothing. Sex didn't have to mean anything. This wasn't love and she didn't have to pretend it was. She could do it and then never see him again.

It didn't have to be a big deal. People had one-night stands all of the time. She sat on the couch and found herself curling into the fetal position.

She didn't know how many hours she lay there agonizing over the proposition, and every once and a while thinking of Taron and how she would tell Hana to not do it, that it wasn't worth the money.

Taron would never let her go through with it, but Hana loved what she did. She saw the reward in the faces of children who'd had no hope of education and advancement turn into joy and promise for their future. That was worth the money. It was worth every black penny of Adrian's money.

Sex was just sex.

She repeated that to herself a couple times then thought about the two lovers she'd had. Robert had been her boyfriend in college, and was a little more experienced than she was—he'd gotten laid a few times, and she'd fooled around in high school but never went "all the way"— which worked. Their mutual fumbling kept the embarrassment factor down. They learned together, and he was a sweet, gentle lover. She started dating Findlay a couple of years out of college, and he was surer of himself than Robert and taught her how to let go of her inhibitions. Still, there was an emotional investment with both guys, and the concept of sex was just sex never crossed her mind.

Switching her thought process to mind over matter, she had to acknowledge Adrian was only asking for sex. It hadn't occurred to her to date him, and she knew there would never be any emotional investment from either of them. Not what she was looking for, and not what she wanted *at all*, but he was making her an offer she was starting to feel like she couldn't refuse. *Ten million dollars.*

So many pencils in so many schools she could build all over the world. She could pay her employees, the rent for the office and her tiny apartment. She'd probably be homeless if she couldn't raise any money from donors.

Adrian's numbers danced in front of her. She'd be crazy to consider it, but she kept replaying the conversation in her mind.

Anytime I want you. The words sent shivers down her spine. What if he wanted her for more than one night? She didn't know what she'd do then. His offer cheapened her, though it was a hell of a lot of money.

It wasn't about the number, but that he thought he could ask her that all. He'd tried to convince her he'd make the experience pleasant, but nothing could make sex for money pleasing. He didn't have to be good in bed, and she didn't have to enjoy it. With ten million dollars, Hana could right Bianca's wrongs.

Even if having sex with Adrian was intolerable, she could see no other option.

By the time night fell, she'd resigned herself to agree to Adrian's proposal. She realized she'd have to hurry because men like him had a short attention span. She had no clue how many women he propositioned per night, but he was filthy rich, and clearly easily bored. He hadn't mentioned keeping the offer open indefinitely.

Hana would consider herself stupid for turning down ten million dollars. She tried to be ruthlessly practical and suppressed her doubts. She couldn't overthink this. She texted his phone number that she read from the crumpled card.

I'll do it.

She sent the text before she had time to regret the words and take them back. He sent a response immediately. She felt the skip in her pulse when she saw three bubbles immediately.

I'm available now.

Then he gave her his address at one the city's most expensive high-rises, of course, and told her he'd leave a pass key for her at the security desk.

That quickly, her fate was sealed. She dropped the phone into her lap and put her head in her hands.

Hana hated him, but she hated herself more. She took a shower and dried her hair. She refused to put on makeup, but wore one of her better dresses.

She knew he would get exactly what he was paying for, but nothing more groomed than the basics. She put on a serviceable pair of matching black underwear. She refused to prepare for this disgusting rendezvous as if it was a sought-after sexy encounter. She held her shoulders back and head high as she hailed a contracted car to take her to his house at 181 Fremont Street.

Of course, it was the top floor apartment with the view she'd imagined he'd own. She had no doubt this penthouse was overpriced and unattainable. She tried to bury any trepidation she had deep inside as she stepped into the elevator and went to his floor. It felt like her life had forever changed when she decided to come.

She was wearing a plum rose pea coat which she hugged to herself. Underneath she wore her beloved cerulean blue wrap dress. It had felt like a comforting choice. Now she realized she'd probably want to burn her favorite clothes after. She refused to back down and shook her fist against the door a couple times. The banging reverberated through the hallways, and she hoped through the floors. Let his paid companion wake up his snobby neighbors.

He let her in immediately, and Hana walked through the door of the most luxurious apartment she had ever been in. She ignored Adrian completely and stepped inside. Hana pretended they were having the office meeting again. This was all business.

She studied the carefully decorated home, which was reminiscent of expensive hotel rooms she'd been in. A decorator's touch was evident with oversized white couches and dark wood furniture. The living room could easily fit a hundred people, and space this size in this city was worth a premium. She could tell every fabric was curated and every book, plant, and bowl were hand selected to adorn the living room. There was absolutely no personality in the room, but the effect was elegant.

Hana walked past the fireplace to the wall to wall window overlooking the bay. His apartment was a 180-degree view of the San Francisco skyline, East Bay, the Bay Bridge, and the Golden Gate Bridge. The view alone was worth five million dollars, she'd stake her life on it. She threw off her coat onto the bone white leather couch and walked up to the window.

She looked over the city she loved, the lights of the highrises shining through the floor to ceiling window as she pressed her hands on the glass. She was probably ruining it with smudges, but she didn't care.

The oils on her fingertips left an ephemeral, if not indelible mark on the glass.

Chapter Six

Adrian joined her at the window. He could tell she was nervous. He could see her shivering. It wasn't cold in his apartment, the flames from the fireplace were a roaring reflection on the window. Hana put on a brave face and an indifferent air, but it was an act.

Hana Romero was in over her head. She was the sweet and innocent face for a charity that built schools for children. Now she was in his apartment about to give away everything that was sweet and innocent about her. He was taking advantage of a selfless woman because he could, and no moral high ground would deter him from this course.

He knew he could make her feel good. Ever since that night they'd danced in City Hall, Adrian could not get the feeling of Hana's body out of his mind. He was used to feelings of casual lust, but his obsession with her bordered on fanatical. Some part of him liked to think he was doing this for philanthropic reasons, but in his heart of hearts he knew it was because of desire.

It was the same desire he was feeling now watching her stare out his window. The city view had that effect on him too, but this view was even more spectacular. She hugged her arms around herself and he studied the curve of her face. Those full kissable lips and hopelessly lost brown eyes.

He liked the way her dark eyebrows crunched as she studied the view. Her black curls fought for dominance over her shoulders and looked romantically tousled. She was untouched by makeup and the expensive gown that she wore the night of the gala. Hana didn't need any of that, she was naturally and unconsciously the sexiest woman who had entranced him.

She put a spell on him and made him unable to move for fear of her leaving his view. He gazed at the fullness of her round bottom leading up to her hips that dipped generously on her slender waist. She made his body tingle with awareness. Like a song he couldn't get out of his head, he kept imagining what he could do with the body of a goddess.

They both could have pleasure. He promised himself he would give her pleasure, and Adrian would finally be satiated by the infernal curiosity of wanting to bed her. He could write the night off as a ten-million-dollar mistake. He never wanted a woman longer than a night. He'd stake a fortune to remove this distraction from his life. Normally he'd care to see where ten million dollars ended up, but he actually trusted Hana would use it to build schools. There seemed to be no loser in this situation.

"Hana," he called in a calm, low voice.

He missed her laughter and her smiling face. He realized she didn't have much to smile about these days. He put a hand on her waist, and she started visibly. She looked so small and alone staring out his window.

He had an annoying thought that someone should have been with her, protecting her from men like him. He reminded himself she chose to be here, and she was a grown and consenting adult. Adrian moved away from her to put her at ease, and walked over to the kitchen, pulled out a newer vintage red wine, and poured a glass for each of them.

He walked back and silently offered her one. She saw the glass in the reflection and turned. She took one of the glasses silently and drank it down while he watched her. He had no need for liquid courage, and sipped the wine.

She was beautiful, he thought, even with her eyes puffy from crying and her hair falling wildly around her shoulders. He liked the put together Hana, but this was Hana here, now, and in his apartment. His urge to kiss her replaced any lingering feelings of guilt he might've had. He wanted her out of that dress too. He walked over to his bag on the dining table and pulled out a contract that he'd had made.

Adrian hadn't been sure at all that she'd say yes, but he'd wanted to put together a serious offer when he did decide to ask. The contract was generous. Ten million dollars as they had agreed, with little to no strings attached. He wanted her to spend some of the money on herself and update her wardrobe if she wished. Not because she looked particularly shabby, but he noticed she didn't spend any money on it.

He knew other non-profit CEOs who tended to make salaries well into the seven figures. He guessed Hana took a modest income. With the papers held firmly in his hand he walked back to the window. She had set the empty glass on the table next to the couch and had returned to her solitary position staring through the window. He held up the packet and silently asked her to take them. She looked at him with hard eyes.

"Have your lawyers look over this," he said.

Hana didn't respond or take the papers from his hands.

"Hire one if necessary and I'll pay," he told her.

Adrian really wanted her to say yes and could see himself being with her so clearly. He'd kiss those lips senseless until she was calling his name, not in anger but in pleasure. He knew he could take her there and felt his need rising yet again.

Only this woman could distract him so and make him completely and embarrassingly occupied with his thoughts of her. He couldn't sleep or eat without thinking of her. He begged her to take the papers and make the fixation go away. He dropped his hand with the papers from the air. She wasn't going to take them.

Instead, she looked up at him and asked, "Would you consider it fair?"

He cocked his head and considered her carefully. "It depends on what you call fair." To make this persistent infatuation go away, priceless.

Ten million dollars was a pittance. He was losing more thinking about her every day. The truth was he made hundreds of millions a year, and last week he lost more money sitting at his desk staring at his computer being unable to function except for thinking about the sting of not having her. He didn't understand it. It was not as though a woman had never refused him.

He had been refused and merrily sent on his way many times by a disinterested woman. Except when Hana had laughed at him and said she would not date him for ten million reasons in the world, he found himself torn up that he couldn't have her.

There were plenty of attractive women who would love to sleep with him. He had been with a fair portion of them, but the black-haired beauty who mocked him had him waking up in the middle of the night and wondering what it would take to be with her.

More than a few times, he couldn't go back to sleep and found himself tossing in a pile of twisted sheets. Then he'd seen the news, as had everyone else, and learned of her misfortune. His wretched dreams turned into lurid fantasies.

He could have her after all. He could have her anytime he wanted.

Hana walked over and stood next to him. She refused to meet his eyes.

She was still on edge when she said, "Am I allowed to say no ever?"

His head reared back in response. He realized she had real concerns about consent. He knew she had no way to trust him, trust that he would never hurt her, but that was not his intention. He wanted to have sex with her, but not without leaving them both satisfied, and, he prayed, cured of this unrelenting desire.

He had seen the flashes of craving in her eyes. She was the type of woman who liked to wait, and maybe he had hoped he was the type of man she might have considered waiting for. She liked his physique maybe, or maybe he knew nothing about Hana at all. He understood this confusion was the price for contracting a woman in such a way. There were no romantic overtures or first nervous kisses building to more arduous ones. He was asking her to go all the way, with no expectation of foreplay or any foreseeable pleasure. But Adrian promised himself and her he would ensure she enjoyed it.

"I would never force you," he stated. "You *must* be a willing participant," he insisted. Offering her a large sum of money forced her hand, of course, but he had no intention of making this anything but a pleasurable experience. He continued in a lower voice. "I don't mean any insult when I say this probably won't last an entire year."

He wanted to satisfy his curiosity at least once, but the words sounded harsh to even his ears. He had never felt more like a monster.

She sent him a pointed glance. "You're making me have sex with you for money," she said angrily, her eyebrows fiercely clenched.

He couldn't disagree with her, but she could leave if she wanted. She didn't have to do this if she didn't want to.

Adrian shrugged her off. "I'm not making you do anything. I think you're genuinely going to use the money to build schools. I think you're doing this because you believe in your charity. I know what I'm getting here. I want you to read this and negotiate," he said holding the contract up for her to take.

The life and spit fire seemed to return. The set of her lips and the look in her eyes said she was determined. She said, "No. I don't need to. You said ten million dollars."

He nodded. "Yes, yours to dictate where you want."

She nodded too, game now for negotiation. He liked her better this way.

"I'll choose my salary—"

He interrupted her quickly. "Capped at one million, minimum."

He really would insist that she use the salary. Maybe he could convince her to buy some lingerie. Maybe he would buy some for her regardless. He imagined what she was wearing under that little wrap dress now.

She spoke more firmly. "I dictate my salary."

He didn't care what she was wearing at this point. He wanted her in his bed now and he could tell she was starting to capitulate. Hang the lingerie.

"Fine," he responded shortly.

It was her money. He didn't care what she did with it. She could waste it all tomorrow, though he knew she wouldn't.

"Fine," she repeated. "Do you have a pen?"

Adrian wished she'd have a lawyer review it. He was silent as she took the contract. He stood there hoping she would at least read through it. It detailed how many sexual encounters were expected, what would happen if she decided to terminate the relationship and what would happen if she spoke of their agreement. She could argue with any point and he'd probably change it for her.

She flipped the pages violently to the last page without glancing at a single word.

"Do you want me to sign or not?"

Adrian nodded and walked over to a desk where he kept his writing utensils. He picked one at random, returned, and offered her the pen. This emotion was new. It was more than guilt. It was acceptance that he was the worst kind of man. He was the kind of man who went through with evil intentions and had women sign away something that was intangible, and in some ways indescribable.

He watched her sign with her hand visibly shaking.

She stilled the tremor and finished her signature.

"What now?" Hana asked, sounding courageous but looking wary.

Adrian realized how brave she was trying to be. He knew she didn't want to sleep with him right now. She wanted and deserved romance and seduction, but now that he had her he wasn't going to stop.

"Follow me," he said.

Chapter Seven

Adrian walked ahead of her toward his bedroom. As soon as she heard him say follow him, it foreshadowed her mistake. She hadn't even read the words she'd signed. Now she was pursuing the devil deeper down into the levels of his wicked inferno.

She couldn't help but marvel how depraved rich men like Adrian were while in the pursuit of entertainment. She was playing a hedonistic game which threatened her life while Adrian's portrait in the attic never changed. Hana wondered if he would tip her if she did a good job. She also wondered when she'd put herself up for auction for him.

She didn't know Adrian at all, but she was taking his hand again. The first time, she'd taken it to have him lead her in a dance, this time he was taking her to his bedroom. Her hand felt so tiny as he took it in his.

The deal with the devil was done, and he was leading her into the bedroom. She took her heels off at the doorway and let go of his hand. He sat down on the bed and rested his hand behind him waiting patiently, and, she realized, he wanted to watch her undress.

She shook her head in a humorous understanding. Hana expected absolutely no less from Adrian Douglas. This act wouldn't be done in the dark and under the covers. The California king sunk under his weight as he sat down on the edge and waited. She saw the dark gray sheets under the warm light of his crystal lamps on either side of the room and imagined they had to a million thread-count.

He was every bit of excess and traveled in a world she'd never experienced. He was Ivy League and bespoke suits. She was state college and Marshall's. He took off his suit jacket and tie with measured care then threw them on the floor. Hana would stake a million of her ten million dollars he paid someone to pick up that jacket.

Her eyes never left his eyes as she took the tie of her dress and pulled at the loose bow. Her wrap dress came apart, and she pulled it off her shoulders. In this space there was no room for modesty. He'd paid for this. For her.

She let his eyes take liberties with her person as they dropped to her breasts, her little tummy, and the curve of her hips. She didn't hide herself with her hands. She was in the light of his perusal, and he raptly looked from one part of her body to another, and then looked back to her eyes. She felt like she was the star of a private sex show.

He was seeing her the way only two boyfriends ever had. She unhooked the clasps and took off the black satin bra with hands that were so still she felt like a surgeon. She refused to let him see her tremble. The bra fell off her fingertips with one deliberate release as her breasts tumbled free.

She'd always loved her breasts, and now Adrian got to see them too. It was the most nerve wracking moment of her life. They were larger than most women's, and she had to admit, she liked the asset. She was unashamed of her body. Her rosy brown nipples were hard against the air as she stood in front of him in only her panties.

Adrian could see every imperfection, every single part of her. He took off his shirt, and she took her fill of his body. He was lean, like she'd thought he'd be. The white fabric of his shirt floated to the ground. He was matching her lack of clothing.

She looked at his chest, the muscled pecs leading to his tapered hips. The crests of his pelvis were narrow, and she followed the vee of his hips as they disappeared into his pants. There wasn't a stitch of fat on that toned male body. He looked like a statue carved out of muscle.

His arms were thickly corded with veins and flexed as he rested his hands on the bed behind him. He resumed his indolent pose as he focused his gaze back on her. His sensuous mouth formed into a slow smile, and his green eyes positively glowed as he looked triumphantly at every part of her body.

The hairs stood up all over her skin. It was an endlessly long moment as they studied each other's naked chests. She felt entitled to study his and unashamed as he looked at hers. She had never had a man devour her visually the way he was right now.

She could tell through the lines of his suit pants that he was hard, and she hated that a part of her desired him a little. She was anticipating the act to come with a small twinge between her thighs. Her sick mind reminded her she liked the way he looked.

He had that pretty boy face with a model's body. He also had arms that could hold her tightly. Those arms were more muscled then she imagined and remembered from that night. She admitted she'd been attracted to Adrian from the start, but she didn't want him this way. Without romance, without words.

She was in no-man's land, hiding in the bunkers as the bombs burst around her. There would be no love tonight. As she started to take off her underwear, she saw he was taking off his pants. He unbuttoned the small black clasp and slipped them over his hips. She could see his engorged penis in boxer briefs.

He was larger than she imagined. In another world she might have wanted to be in his bed, but tonight she was reluctant. Each newly exposed patch of skin tingled with awareness of his steady and constant gaze. Her hair hung down her back, and she realized she hadn't had a wax between her thighs in weeks. The dark curls were untamed.

She imagined that most of his girlfriends were bare, but she had a wax trim, and she would refuse to do go bare for him. She was truly naked and subject to his criticism. She hadn't been with anyone in a while and she felt anticipation building. She tried to look away from his burning gaze, but she couldn't.

Adrian stood up, wearing only his boxer briefs. He began to walk to her, and Hana felt like the world was crashing in on her. She wanted to run. She was so acutely aware she was naked and he was coming nearer. She knew he was about to kiss her, and she stood her ground. His bed was looming behind him, and it was all she could look at.

This could have been after a date, the two of them naked and about to consummate whatever romance they had started. Except this was no affair of the heart. He reached out and put his hands in her hair. Her scalp tingled as he ran his fingers through the long curls. She couldn't help it, she looked down at the plush white carpet and shivered with the intimidating nearness of him. At the thick wall of muscled chest standing in front of her, and those massive fingers smoothly combing her hair. His touch was gentle, but his up-close and in-person presence was startling. As he stroked her hair, all she could hear was her own breathing and the soft combing sounds.

Every second he didn't touch her body built the anticipation as he let her feel his presence. She gradually accepted his nearness and determinedly looked up into his eyes. She waited for his next move. He smiled again as he moved his hands up to the base of her scalp. It was then Adrian finally kissed her.

With his hand on the crown of her head, he secured her and crushed his lips to hers in possessive fire. They were molten on hers, moving her to kiss him back. His lips were soft, but his body was hard, and Hana found herself giving as good as she got. She told herself it was to make it go faster, but she found the longer he kissed her the more she wanted him to kiss her. She felt the same feverish intensity he'd promised with his eyes in his kiss.

His lips were like fire against her mouth, and he invaded her with his tongue. If she pretended he was her boyfriend, she would have enjoyed this kiss. It was a kiss full of discovery, and was brutal and shocking. She started to put her hands on him almost to control him but at the same time to stop the intensity. She put her fingers on each side of his face to try to grab him in her hands.

But trying to control Adrian was like trying to control the raging sea and he was kissing her in a way that showed his skill. He didn't have to tell her how many women he had been with. His expert kiss belied how good he was at this. He continued to kiss her. He hadn't even touched her yet, but she was feeling things in her breasts and between her legs she hadn't expected. He made her feel his need, and it became hers too.

The desire started as an uncontrollable twinge. She didn't want to feel attracted to him, but she kept kissing him as he pressed her against his body. Her breasts were crushed against his hard chest. He was making her want him, one aching advance at a time. Then he put his hands on her body for the first time.

His hand gripped the back of her waist the same as when they were dancing, and she felt that way again. Adrian and his intense kiss wrapped her up and left her breathless. She pulled away and his hand slipped to her crux of her hip. She was so aware of him, his nearness and his hands on her body. It burned where he touched.

She thought she'd be more nervous, but she slipped her arms around his neck like they were dancing again. This time she pulled him into the kiss. There was a heady power in turning the table on him. To make his lips accept her kiss and her need as she pushed him. She found them moving toward his bed as he kissed her back.

So, this was how bad boys kissed, she mused. She'd never kissed one and she definitely knew it now. This was how the devil kissed once you'd agreed to let him sleep with you.

As she fell against the sheets of his bed, she found herself tangled in a mix of limbs. She felt one greedy hand take possession of her breasts. The gentle massage sent waves of pleasure down her body. She didn't want to love it, but she loved the way his large hands cupped her. He had one nipple in his fingers as he gently pinched.

As she gasped, he took back control of her mouth with an open-mouthed kiss. His tongue played with hers and she tasted the wine and the flavor of him. His hands roamed all the places he'd looked at before. He caressed her hips and moved to cup her ass. He was pulling her against him and at the same time her legs fell open for him to find a place to rest on her.

Adrian settled between her legs and his hardness pressed against her. He was unrelenting male need and flagrant desire ready to claim her. She shivered as his hands left her breasts. He took his mouth away from her swollen lips to claim her body too. His mouth traveled from the sensitive spot on her neck to the top swell of her breast. He was looking at her again, like she was his, like he owned her.

She reminded herself that he couldn't own her but shut her eyes when he put that sinful mouth on one tortured nipple. It was aching as he pulled it into his mouth and sucked gently. He was taking his time, and the desire pooled in her belly. She couldn't help the response. He was turning her on, one carnal kiss at a time.

Those lips were punishing as he took the tip of her breast into his mouth. The skin reacted under his attention. She squirmed against the pleasure. She knew what it meant when her body reacted this way.

She desired him. She kept having the intense feeling that something was building up inside of her. She could feel his large cock rubbing against her in the most insistent way. She thought about it being inside of her while his wicked hands touched her. They were silent and the only sounds were his mouth on her.

She released a sigh of frustration she'd been holding as the tips of his fingers rubbed her where she ached most. He was making this easy at least. They had desire and now pleasure. She told herself she didn't have to hate every moment of it.

Hana let him make her feel good, and the pressure of his hand rubbing against her aching sex caused the waves of pleasure she needed. All the tension faded away in his arms. He took her mouth again as he massaged her. His fingers rubbed her clit insistently, with frustrating familiarity to the path of gratification. He knew right where to touch to make it feel like intimacy, like unrelenting passion.

She could feel his eyes on her. He was looking at her again as his hand pleasured her between her thighs, but she didn't care. She had the indulgence he was giving her, and he could watch her find her release if he wanted. He knew exactly what to give her, and he quickened the tempo of his fingers with expert ease.

She felt the rising of an orgasm burgeoning between her thighs and couldn't help but scream against his mouth. It took her by surprise this orgasm. But any contentment Hana took away from it was gone as she opened her eyes to look into the devilish green gaze looking down at her. Adrian was ready to take his satisfaction too and he released himself from his underwear. Again, she realized how big he really was.

She'd never been with a lover like this. She'd never been with someone this hard. Physically, he was all tight muscles. As she ran her hands appreciatively along his arms, she was slow with her fingers and unapologetic. Hana took her time. She'd already found her satisfaction. She wanted to touch him now.

She put her hand on his firm chest. Adrian took no prisoners and gave no softness. The muscles of his abs bounced as she dragged her hand lower. He pulled back from her. Those emerald eyes again staring into her soul, daring her to turn back.

He looked at her and waited. Hana was still panting a little at the feeling of intensity of her gratification, but one look from Adrian and the excitement built up again.

Hana nodded. She felt his absence everywhere as Adrian got up and went to his bedside table.

Chapter Eight

Adrian replayed every steaming hot moment in his mind. Hana on his bed, completely naked while he made her come. Hana screaming into his mouth. He'd never been more turned on in his life. Any regret he had in making the proposition vanished when she pulled that dress off her shoulders.

She'd stood there bravely in her black bra and panties, never backing down for a second. He had anticipated wanting her, but as she took off her clothes, she tortured him with the tease of revealed skin. This was everything he had imagined when he saw her walking down the City Hall stairs in her black dress.

Adrian finally had her, even though he'd made a dark bargain to do it.

He would never forget the sight of Hana staring back at him as she unclasped her bra and dropped it on his floor. He stared at that perfect body of hers. Her breasts were gorgeous and round and looked like everything soft and female. He had never known a woman like her. The full breasts led to the natural curve of her waist and then flared out to her hips. She was sexy in a way no other woman could be.

Hana was courageous and unintimidated, holding herself in front of him. She didn't flinch as he looked at his fill. He took off his clothes eagerly. He still couldn't believe how much he wanted this woman. He realized part of it was her innate goodness. The moral graciousness radiated off of her. The only reason she was dropping her panties on his carpet was because he was the bad man who'd promised her money to do it. He had realized at the gala that Hana believed every word she was saying.

She was going to use this money to help her schools, and she was going to save the world. She didn't want anything more from him than that. But her orgasm, her pleasure, and the telling way she panted for breath as he touched her was all him. He was proud of the way he'd made her cry out. He wanted this to feel good for her, even if it wasn't. He knew nothing he'd done was right, but something felt so right when he kissed her.

When they were dancing, he'd gotten over the initial fascination of her beauty and seen the intriguing woman underneath. Her eyes were shining as she talked about Esperanza and they were shining now, glazed over by passion. He liked her like this, full of intoxication for him, her chest rising deeply as she let herself feel. He liked giving her pleasure. His hands could do it, and he was helpless to close his eyes when he could watch her scream out in climax.

He grabbed a condom from his nightstand. He was too eager for this. He wanted this insatiable need to go away. He knew once he'd had her he'd be satisfied. He never wanted to be with a woman more than one night, and even though he was so hard it hurt right now, he doubted Hana would be anything different.

Adrian rejoined her in bed and looked at her again. Time and time again he wondered about what kind of deal he'd made. Ten million dollars. It wasn't about the money, but what they were about to do. The look on her face was determined. Hana was no innocent about sex, though she was in other ways.

She was no seasoned sex worker. She was a woman who'd probably been with only a few guys at the most. His throat working, he realized he was about to be one of them. He couldn't stop himself from the flash of guilt that came over him. It didn't stop his erection and it didn't stop him from kissing her, but it was in the back of his mind.

He was going to take her, even if he felt like shit about it tomorrow. He put his hand on her breast again. He didn't get tired of the feeling of those gorgeous mounds in his hands. They were made for his touch, even larger than what could fit in his palm. He massaged her back to the frenzy he wanted her in.

He liked it when she kissed him back and he could tell she was ready. She was so wet, it dripped on the sheets and he knew she was primed for him. He rolled the condom on quickly. He got on top of her and stilled over her. He wanted to give her a moment to back out, one last time before he made her his.

Adrian knew he couldn't own her, but he certainly felt a glimpse of what it would be like with a woman like Hana. He was looking down at her and those big brown eyes were looking up at him. Her lips were swollen and well used, and her hands were all over him. Adrian wanted to tell her where he wanted her hands, but he allowed her to have them on his chest, on his arms, and in his hair. He settled back into the cradle of her hips and positioned himself at her entrance.

There was no going back now. She didn't say anything, and he almost stopped. Then she kissed him, and he knew he couldn't. He couldn't stop now any more than he could stop the rain. He pushed forward with a gentle thrust. She was wet and tight around the tip of his cock and he crushed the urge to push further.

He was sliding into her so slowly he could feel every inch of her as it swallowed him whole. Hana was so tight around him, he gasped. It was the most exquisite torture he'd ever experienced. As she adjusted to his hard length he kept going. She was kissing him and the electricity of her lips on his was so intense he closed his eyes and completed the thrust.

He was completely sheathed, and it felt like ignited fire in his groin. She was everything he knew she would be. Sweet and tender, it almost felt like making love. His hips were seated in the cradle of hers when he moved. Gentle at first, but he slid out of her and then slid back in before she missed the shaft of his cock.

He wanted to take his time here too, but the pleasure was building. Adrian felt like he was becoming unmanned every time he took himself out of her then put himself back in. It was so hot he couldn't stand it. Every second was perfect as he swallowed her moans of pleasure. It was the sounds coming from her mouth that were putting Adrian over the edge. He wanted more and he grabbed her legs and put them over his shoulder.

***

When Adrian rolled on the condom, Hana hadn't expected the night to go like this. She was turned on from looking at him and anticipating what would happen next. Every second of it had been surprising. It was astonishing how easy it was to pretend he wasn't her boyfriend. To forget that this was all for ten million dollars.

Adrian was wicked with those hands, and he made her feel things she had never felt. She hated how easy the pleasure came. Hana always thought she needed love to enjoy sex. Boy, was she wrong.

As he thrust into her, she had felt him stretching her gloriously. His thick cock drove into her again and again. The walls of her vagina had clung to him as his unrelenting need pushed her over the edge. At first, he'd gone slow, and she'd felt the pleasure building up again, then he increased the pace.

He was rough with her, and she rode the pleasure waves as long as she could before she gasped. She was going to come again. She was absolutely bewildered when he fucked her into a second orgasm, holding her legs over his shoulders. This position made every push deeper, and she was screaming now with every movement.

***

Adrian was happy he could take her there. She was matching him thrust to thrust with her round bottom slapping against his hips as he rode her. When he felt her climaxing, he savored every moment of her delicious screams. The tightening of her pussy around him milked an orgasm from him unwillingly. He was going to come, and he couldn't help it. The waves of pleasure rolled over him with the sweet release of ecstasy. The intensity of it stole his breath and every thought from his mind. Hana pervaded every sense he had.

***

Hana felt the ripples of pleasure as he shouted his release, then he collapsed on top of her. She couldn't help it, she let herself feel hers too. At least he made wrong feel good. Hana closed her eyes as they lay joined for a couple moments, waiting for her heart to calm down.

He rolled off of her and she felt bereft. Hana was quiet next to him as she panted for breath. Adrian caught a couple breaths too before getting up and heading to the bathroom. She appreciated the moment to collect her thoughts. She felt strange lying alone in his bed. It was an intimate setting, and she didn't know him. Well, she certainly knew him better than she had a half hour ago.

She had only danced with him, barely even talked to him. They'd spent more words arguing in his office than getting to know each other. She had never even been on one date with him, and she was a ten-date kind of girl. Hana had to come face to face with several realizations. She'd had amazing sex with Adrian Douglas.

It shouldn't've been that good. But as pleasurable as it had been, the act was over now. Hana couldn't believe she'd gone through with it. She couldn't take the night back if she wanted to. She didn't know what to feel.

She'd given him her body for money, and it had been enjoyable, more than it should have been. She sat up and held the sheet to her body, her hair a tossed mess about her head. She patted her hair down and hung onto the satin sheet, preserving a small shred of modesty and shyness even though he'd seen her completely naked. She realized the worst part about the sex was that after it was over, a quiet panic settled over her.

Hana dreaded him returning from the bathroom but refused to run away from the encounter. She was no coward, though she had no clue what to do now that the deed was done. She waited for him to walk to the doorway and she found his nakedness startling. Adrian was pure male, and even flaccid, he was still throwing off serious sex vibes.

She didn't know what to say, so she turned to look at the fireplace. She wanted to leave but she didn't want to seem like a coward. Taron always told her to never let them see beneath your armor. Never let them see you cry.

She kind of wanted to cry now, but she'd be damned if he saw her that way.

Chapter Nine

"I'm going to go," Hana declared as he watched her from the doorway.

She dropped the sheet bravely. He looked as she knew he would, and she fought the urge to cover herself up. He was an animalistic passion even now. He was standing there completely naked and didn't cover any of his exposed parts as she collected her clothes off the floor.

Adrian nodded. "Call me tomorrow," he ordered as she began to put on her clothes.

He disappeared into a closet without her reply. She was thankful. As she clasped her bra and put on her panties, she was stunned by the passion filled night. But she regretted it. She wished she hadn't done it, but she couldn't forget the feeling of his hands on her.

Even now, she could tell by the way he'd looked at her, he would have had her again. Adrian was unapologetic and she would have to comfort herself with nothing but cold hard cash. She could never tell Taron, much less her mother as long as she lived. She would keep this secret forever.

She didn't wait for him to reappear. She grabbed up her shoes, made her way back to the living room, grabbed her coat and finished putting herself together in the hallway. She walked outside of his high-rise and onto the street, hugging her peacoat to herself as she had when she'd arrived.

Except now she had a vivid memory stuck in her brain.

Adrian on top of her, possessing her. Adrian kissing her.

It was all she could do to look at the lights of the buildings above her and collect a breath. An older man approached her in a suit, he looked old enough to be her grandfather, but he was acting like a perfect gentleman when he opened the door of a sleek black vehicle. His silver head bowed as he spoke and he held out his other hand for her in invitation. "Ms. Romero, I know you don't know me, but my name is Louis." He smiled kindly. "I work for Mr. Douglas."

She shook her head and took his open palm in a firm handshake. Models in penthouses and drivers waiting around the block. She hadn't been wrong about the things she'd assumed about Adrian. Except how his kiss would feel. She'd been surprised about that.

"Hana," she corrected. "My name is Hana."

"I prefer Ms. Romero if it's the same to you," he said. She respected him for it. "Mr. Douglas was hoping you would let me drive you home. I would be honored if you'd let me."

She bridled at Adrian's impertinence, but didn't have the energy to say no. Hana nodded.

"Thank you, Mr. Louis," she said, and then recited her address.

Hana laughed quietly to herself as he closed the door behind her. She recognized the make and model of the vehicle as a Rolls Royce Phantom. It was easily a half million-dollar car, and she had never even ridden in one before. It was all she could do not to laugh, or cry.

She didn't want to cry until she got home to her apartment.

She could almost believe this had been a date, but they hadn't done any date things. Only sex.

When they arrived at her address she thanked Louis again as he opened the door for her. The idea of a personal driver and luxury cars gave further testament to how wealthy Adrian must be. The kind of wealth he could throw away on one night of sex. He didn't blink at the ten-million-dollar figure or at taking her to his bed.

She walked inside and slammed the door behind her, dropping a trail of her clothing on the floor and slipped into her sheets. She shut her eyes tightly and refused to think for even a moment. Surprisingly, she felt herself falling asleep.

When she woke and opened her eyes, it felt like the hours passed in mere seconds. She didn't feel rested at all.

She was completely distracted as she got dressed and walked all the way to her office. She sat alone at her desk, staring out her window. She was supposed to be working. Some of the employees had already returned, and she saw them pass back and forth through the open doorway like they were in another universe. Taron poked her head into the room and checked on her occasionally.

When she'd told her friend of Adrian's donation, Taron hadn't questioned it. She knew men like him made millions of dollars at his lunch hour. Naively, she thought he was philanthropic.

Hana told Taron that Adrian had donated one million and kept the other nine a secret. She had never kept a secret from her best friend, and she resented the intrusion of secrecy in their relationship. Now Adrian was invading the oldest friendship in her life. She had never kept anything from Taron, maybe her mother, but not from Taron.

As Hana replayed the night in her mind she decided he wasn't really generous. He was generous with his mouth, his hands, his cock, his money, and the time he spent with her, but not with his heart.

Adrian Douglas had no heart. He was a bad man.

Still she admitted that he made it easy to be bad, paving the road with kisses that burned like a thousand fires and the promise of climax even though it was against her will. She accepted that she'd bedded him for the money and everything that meant. It was worth the look on Taron's face to realize that Esperanza wasn't going under. She hugged her friend extra tight and was glad to be with her.

"That was generous of Mr. Douglas," Taron remarked, sitting across from her as Hana stared out the window.

She'd been helplessly caught up in the movie theater in her own head. She looked through the window and focused on the rugged urban landscape. She didn't have a particularly nice view, but it was hers. She used to like the view, but right now she found it unsettling. Maybe that was the effect he'd had on her. She would never be able to recover from this deal she'd made with him. Even if she gave the money back, she'd never be able to unlive last night.

Hana murmured her agreement. She was thinking about the way he threw his shirt to the floor, the way she'd taken her clothes off in front of him. She had been completely exposed, naked and vulnerable in his apartment. She had never had sex with a man she didn't love.

Adrian had watched her strip and when he walked over to her, he wasn't wearing anything but his boxer briefs. Then he kissed her. He kissed her like a storm of passion and desire, and Hana had responded to his kiss. She had willed herself to accept what pleasure he could give, and it haunted her now.

Taron talked again, and Hana focused her attention on her friend. "I saw you guys dancing," Taron said. "Clearly, we made quite the impression on him."

Taron was thinking of the night of the ball, while Hana was thinking about the night of the proposition. The handsome prince had come to find her, but he hadn't proposed marriage. There would be no glamorous Cinderella adventure with Adrian. Hana was silent. Every night with Adrian had been burned in her mind.

At the gala, she'd passionately spoken for her company, and Taron had too. They still believed in Esperanza. Even though they'd almost lost the company, she was glad to be here today. She'd worn that dress and it had made her feel like she was out for revenge. She had felt so beautiful and sexy.

She liked the way Adrian had paid her attention then, and the way that he held her on the dance floor. If she had said something different, she could have had him without the proposal. Without the indecency. Instead there was ten million dollars hanging between them.

Taron called her by their endearment. "Mami, we have to start planning our next school. I've gotten hundreds of proposals, and I need your help."

Hana snapped to attention at the word proposal. She closed her eyes and opened them slowly. She hadn't called him even though he'd asked her to. He'd told her in his office. *Anytime I want you* he'd said.

She couldn't manage to do it. If he wanted her, he'd call her. He knew her number, he was the one who needed to call. Otherwise she'd have to assume he'd gotten his fill of her and his desire for her sated. She hadn't read the contract, but she started to think she finally understood men like him. He wanted her for the challenge, and now that it was gone she might not hear from him at all.

She startled as her phone rang as if she'd conjured him. It was her mom calling, and she stopped to talk to her. She didn't know any English, so Hana switched to Spanish and talked to her mom for a while, promising many times to come over later. Her mother kept her talking so Taron went back to her office.

Hana continued to repeat her promises for several more minutes as Adrian strolled through the door. She wanted to curse, but she hurried her mother off the phone instead. She stood up and felt like her heart stopped.

"What are you doing here?" she asked out of breath.

She looked over his perfectly cut blond hair and untroubled green eyes. She couldn't dismiss his breathtaking jawline and overly pretty male features. If the devil was so evil, why did he have to look so good in a tailored suit? His jacket was finely fitted against his wide shoulders and the button cinched at his narrowed waist. He had a thick black outer jacket over it, and she guessed it had to be cold out. She hadn't noticed when she walked to the office. She'd been numb since she left his apartment last night.

She didn't look nearly as put together as he did. She was bundled up in a large holey sweater and her favorite distressed blue denims. She had put her hair up in a ballerina bun. Coils of her curls hung about her un-made up face. She couldn't hide her surprise, and lack of sleep had to be evident. She'd seen the bags beneath her eyes in the mirror this morning.

She walked over to him and closed the door. He was the type of man to show up unannounced. He was presumptuous in that way. He looked unbothered as ever and took a seat in front of her desk. She found herself moving to the other side and sitting there, mirroring a conversation they'd had before.

Chapter Ten

"You didn't call," he said in mock censure. It was almost like he was trying to flirt with her.

"No," she replied softly and chuckled. "I didn't."

He blinked at her, like he was resetting, then cocked his head and said, "It's seven. What time do you usually eat?"

The irony didn't escape her. She had to laugh. He could be so ridiculous sometimes. "Are you inviting me to dinner?" she asked incredulously.

The conversation mirrored their first evening together at the gala, and she wondered where they would be if she had said yes to him then. If she had just gone to dinner with him. Instead her dark angel had come to rescue her with more money than she could ever dream of if she gave up her body to him. She felt like a fraud ever since she agreed to his detestable proposal.

"I guess I am," he answered and smiled, a genuine true curve of his lips.

It was striking on that pretty boy brooding face and completely transformed his features. She cocked her head, and remembered something she'd heard in the church her mother had taken her to every Sunday as a child. The devil had been exquisitely beautiful too.

She imagined now he might have looked something like this, crossing his calves indolently and propping his head up on his hand, his elbow on the arm of her chair. Adrian looked most like himself, completely relaxed and at ease. The genuine smile however was new, and its novelty was charming and seemed precious somehow.

She reminded herself that this man was the guy she was sleeping with to pay the bills. She shouldn't fantasize about making him smile. She had no obligation to talk to him at all. Hana ought to demand he never visit her office again. Suddenly he seemed too large and at home in her office. She wanted to kick the arm from under his head.

Hana poked the bear. “Is it in the contract I have to have dinner with you?” She mimicked his office acting performance and tented her fingers under her chin like she was considering him.

He had the audacity to look affronted. “No. I’s not in the contract.”

She still hadn’t read the damn thing. It could stipulate a dinner date before each sexual act. She had no clue what this narcissistic rich boy had spelled out for her. Adrian was a mystery. She wondered why he’d bother with dinner if all he wanted was sex. She wondered why she perked up at the sound of his offer. She didn’t recoil from the thought of him like she should, she found herself wanting to say yes.

“Then I’ll go,” she declared. “I haven’t eaten all day.” She picked up her purse and headed for the door. She wanted to get him out of her office so she waved him on and led the way. “Come on,” she said with a laugh. “I know a place nearby.”

She led him around the corner where they served hot French fries and cold draft beer. She tried not to laugh as she watched him sit gingerly in the old pub chair as if his presence in this establishment was an affront to his outfit. He was so vainglorious it made her laugh. She would love to see if he ever let his hair down. If he ever wore anything but expensive suits. She noticed he cut his fries with a fork and knife and only sipped at his beer.

She was halfway through her second pint and laughing because he looked so serious every time he ordered. Like this was a fine establishment, but he looked out of place. Adrian was funny in some ways, and kind of ridiculous.

“Laugh at me all you want,” he said and smiled. “But I use a fork to eat pizza too.”

He popped a fry into his mouth with his utensil. He looked kind of boyish, even though he was wearing an outrageously expensive adult suit. He had a gleam to his eye and an easiness about him. She could imagine him eating pizza with a fork and a napkin tucked into his black bow tie and tuxedo. He was a man at home in formal wear, and probably more used to drinking at more refined eateries.

She stole a fry with her greasy fingers then licked them clean. She liked the salt granules as they exploded on her tongue.

"You're wrong, Adrian," she insisted. "Some things are finger food."

He watched her lick her fingers then took a slow sip of his beer. Everything was sexual with him, she realized. She felt like he was waiting to pounce on her. His intentions were never innocent when it came to her. He had come to her office because she hadn't called, and he had paid for the privilege of her time.

She realized she never saw him drink more than one drink. He was a man in control of his time, his mind, and his money. And now her.

He'd told her he liked to acquire things. She realized she was another of his acquisitions.

"How was your day?" she asked. She was genuinely curious. What did billionaires do during the daytime when they kept the nights so busy buying women?

He accounted for the time easily. "I sold some property," he said, ticking the list off his fingers. "I took my mother and my sister out for lunch, then I spent the next four hours with my accountant wondering if you would call." He clarified by clearing his throat and dropping his hand. "My accountant wasn't wondering, but I was."

"I didn't want to call," she said, shrugging nonchalantly. While she'd agreed to be with Adrian at any time he wanted for as long as he wanted her, he would have to pursue her, not the other way around.

"How was yours?" he asked.

Hana shook her head. She didn't tell him that she spent the whole day thinking about him. If she closed her eyes, she could pretend that this was the dinner she could have said yes too. She thought of Bianca again and what she'd stolen. She was thinking of why she was even here with him in the first place.

The money. He couldn't possibly care about her day, and she didn't want to care about his. When he'd ask her out at the gala, she'd turned him down for a reason. He required more time and emotional upkeep than she wanted to invest in a man, or in anyone for that matter. There was a reason she didn't have a boyfriend. Taron and their charity were her lovers. She didn't have time for lovers like this.

Adrian was the type of lover who left her breathless, left her wanting more, and while she knew he was a bad man, she was worried she might have a weakness for them. She'd been thinking about the proposal all morning. Then that turned into the memory of her saying yes to sleep with him and what would come next.

She was thinking about saying yes to him again and what that might look like. Here he was in the flesh, asking her now to be with him. She shrugged silently in answer to his question. She didn't have words for the experience.

"Are you available this evening?" he asked, his smile fading into an intense look.

There it was, the next proposal. She knew before long she'd be back in his bed. In a fairy tale he would have been asking her to dance again, or if the story was sappy enough, he'd be asking to marry her. Instead he was asking her to fulfill her part of the bargain.

She nodded but stalled for time. "I want to stop by my apartment."

"Of course," he agreed.

Adrian didn't finish his drink, but he made for his wallet. She moved quicker and put the cash out instead. He'd probably always expected to pay. She didn't mind paying for their meal. She never minded paying for a man's meal, but his insincere attempt at chivalry didn't matter anymore. This wasn't a date whether she wanted it to be or not. She liked to think she would have paid regardless of being in his employ.

"My treat," she insisted and stood up.

He inclined his head and followed suit. As he opened the door for her, she saw Louis pull up. He had uncanny timing, this Louis. She remembered that's what money could buy. She'd never forget, she was one of the things money could buy.

"Same address, Mr. Louis," she said opening the car door for herself and got in.

She waited as Adrian got in the car and sat next to her. She was aware of his nearness and the expectancy of it all. Now that she knew what it would be like, she was nervous all over again. She put her seat belt on with as calm of hands she could manage as Adrian did too. She turned to the window and looked out.

She wondered how many girls had been in this car. How many in his apartment? The thoughts rolled around in her head as the car's wheels rolled through the streets of San Francisco. She wondered how many women he'd bought, and how many had signed one of his contracts.

She opened the door to get out and told him, "I'll be a couple of minutes, if you don't mind waiting." She turned and didn't wait for his reply. She realized she didn't want him going up to her apartment. Her place wasn't anything like the penthouse he lived in. He had white couches and crystal lamps, and she ate with her feet kicked up on her refurbished couch. She didn't even tell Adrian she had a cat.

They lived vastly different lives, and she couldn't imagine clean cut, snobby Adrian in her apartment. He'd wince at the way she lived, and the cat hair would repel him. He wordlessly nodded as she closed the door and headed upstairs, kicking off her shoes and closing the door behind her. She closed her eyes and for a moment pretended she wasn't in this predicament and rested her on the door. She promised herself five minutes of this, just breathing in and out, and processing.

She felt the heady anticipation of desire taking over again. No matter how depraved she knew he was, she couldn't stop replaying last night in her mind. On Adrian's satiny sheets, he'd discovered every secret she could hide with her clothes. Lights on, eyes open. Adrian was larger than life in her mind, in her office and in the car, and she could barely breathe around him.

He'd promised to make her feel pleasure. He'd promised that they'd both enjoy it, and he had been right. She knew he was right. She had never had sex like that. Mind-blowing orgasms that blew every expectation she ever had when she saw him that night in the tuxedo.

Every moment of last night was tainted with the memory of what it meant, what she'd done. She closed her eyes against the world and shut out everything. The memory of Adrian and the feeling of his lips and the morning after, waking up and having known him so intimately. She'd been the billionaire's plaything, his mistress in the penthouse. This morning when she woke, she'd opened her eyes to the ringing cell phone at her bedside.

She flipped through the emails with a hanging headache of the reality of the situation. A private bank was trying to contact her, give her access to her account. She realized Adrian had done that for her. The bank needed more personal information to secure her assets.

With a sinking heart, she knew he had fulfilled his side of the proposition. There were no roses in their relationship, no Shakespeare sonnets on her pillow. If she was expecting Adrian to take music to her window or call her with confessions of love, she was wrong. With every ring of her phone, she realized the only calls she was going to get was from a bank in Switzerland.

The writing was on the wall. She wasn't Cinderella and Adrian wasn't Prince Charming. She had no hope of love after she signed her name with his pen. There could be no illusions. She opened her eyes, but nearly jumped out her skin as she felt the door jiggle.

A firm double knock rang out and startled her so much she grabbed her hair as she opened the doorway. There was Adrian defying her again with his presence. He didn't wait in the car like she'd asked. She didn't get any relief from thoughts of him all day. Here he was in front of her again.

She knew by the look in his eyes, he was going to kiss her.

Chapter Eleven

Hana knew in exactly one second he was about to grab her and kiss her like the black-hearted man he was. It would feel like sin, and it would feel like passion, and it would turn her on like she'd never been in her life. She wished this desire she felt for him was more romantic, slower and more teased out. But this was more intense. He was her indecent Prince Charming.

One second passed like an eternity and Adrian walked up to her and she put her hands on his chest as he captured her lips in a kiss. It was remarkable how though he'd already had her, this kiss felt more intense than the last time. It was like he knew how good it could be so he couldn't get enough. He helped her put her legs around his waist as he slammed the door to her apartment shut with his foot.

***

The slamming door reverberated through the apartment. All the while Hana didn't stop kissing him, and the passion stole Adrian's breath away. He carried her to the one room that had to be her bedroom and laid her on the bed. The apartment looked Hana, colorful and soft, and cluttered and messy and warm at the same time.

She pushed aside a mountain of pillows to the floor. She loved making a mess. He staked his claim and put her in the cage of his arms and kissed her again. Her kisses were like a potent drug where the effect had him wanting to do it again immediately. He took off his suit jacket and threw it on her floor, and then took off his shirt too. She was about to rip it off of him. Her hands were in a frenzy all over his body.

He wanted her to take off that ugly sweater, and she didn't hesitate to comply. She pulled the sweater over her head. He was hard the moment he walked into the apartment. Looking at her lacy white bra made his cock ache with need. He helped her unbutton her jeans and was sucking on her neck while she pulled them down her calves. He already had his hands under the cups of her bra.

She put her hands behind her back to help take it off. Adrian pressed his advantage and put his mouth back on her body. He wanted to kiss every part of her. He bit her gently on the side of her breast and tugged on one free nipple with his teeth. She was calling out in pleasure and her eyes had an unfocused look. He liked that he could make her feel this way, and he intended to work her up so she climaxed around him when he was deep inside her.

***

She wished this thing with Adrian wasn't so complicated. She knew any man who offered her money for passion was a bad man, but the way he kissed her was criminally pleasurable. Good guys didn't rip her clothes off like this and pull her breast in their mouth. A good guy wouldn't look at her like she was his next meal, and he was starving.

Adrian was looking at her as he lay back on her bed. Ever since he barged into her home, she couldn't help but notice how strange he looked in her quirky apartment. Buttoned up in his natural fiber suits as he kissed her in front of her cat. She lived in a shoebox and he was a massive presence inside of it. He took up her entire queen-size bed.

He was shirtless, and she found it funny how innocent he managed to look with his blond hair falling around his eyes. Adrian was the opposite of angelic, yet she appreciated the look of him. He was handsome and had a certain magnetism, and she got to look at him as much as he got to look at her.

She felt his firm biceps under her fingers as she moved to touch his chest, then dragged her hands down his abs and felt his solid male body underneath her. She put her legs on either side of the hips of the gorgeous half-naked man on her bed. Even if they didn't have love, she could admit she desired him. Maybe it was the way the muscles on his chest jumped under her fingers as she trailed them down those muscles. Maybe it was the urge to kiss his soft lips again. She leaned forward and kissed him not waiting for him to kiss her because she wanted to.

Hana pushed his arms above his head demanding him with her actions. He acquiesced and she turned her kiss into a playful bite of his sinful mouth. She took his lip and tugged on it with her teeth. She couldn't deny the desire she was feeling from head to toes.

She wanted Adrian now, and was at least guaranteed to get a little something out of this besides money. She could bet he could make her come again. Something about his perfectly arrogant face made her want to shut him up and keep him busy. She pulled back and away from him.

He was watching her unapologetically and didn't disguise that he was as turned on as she was. She put her fingers on the edge of her underwear and began to pull off her panties. She took her time and made him watch her do it slowly. She reveled in how long she could drag it out even though they both knew where this was going to end.

He didn't blink once and watched raptly as the fabric slipped over her knees. She climbed on top of him and looked down marveling at how she was controlling their play. She wanted to use him as much as he was using her, and he seemed to encourage everything she offered.

She sat on his chest while he massaged her thighs. He was pulling the skin so hard and putting so much pressure on them that she started to feel the blood pooling between her legs.

Desire was turning into aching need. She had been thinking about him all day, and she had been thinking about this. He pushed up on his elbows and bit her inner thigh. He was inviting her to sin, and have mercy, she'd fantasized about that face on her, and under her. She realized she wanted him to eat her, and her face flushed at the thought.

She never wanted someone's mouth on her so badly before in her life. She was talking dirty in her mind. Adrian read her mind and pulled her bottom toward his face. She straddled his head, positioned over his lips.

She screamed when she felt his tongue on her.

He captured the nub of her clitoris in a kiss like he did everywhere else on her body. With unrelenting intensity. She couldn't believe it. Hana was sitting on the pretty boy's face, and he ate her out like she was on the menu and he couldn't get enough.

He had his tongue swirling against her as she pulled her hair out of her bun, spilling out over her shoulders making her feel wilder.

She was going insane. He was doing things with his mouth that threatened her sanity. She was about to come.

He was sucking on her insistently, and Hana felt the pleasure building up. She pulled his fingers up to her breasts, and he started to pull on her nipples. His wicked hands were driving her to madness.

She ground her hips against the sides of his head, pushing herself closer to his mouth and his carnal kiss. His tongue was unyielding, it demanded her submission with insistent flicks. As she rode his face, she came on his mouth. She couldn't stop the waves of pleasure that radiated through her body. Adrian was pure sex.

Her sheets were black, and Adrian looked like a dark angel lying on them, a satisfied smirk on his face. He pushed her into his lap, and she took the liberty of freeing him from his pants. He pulled them over his hips with his underwear and she remembered how big he was with a shuddering surprise.

She closed her eyes as he kissed her again, his tongue slipping into her mouth with heady familiarity. His narcotic kisses were dragging her deeper into the mystery of a man who hadn't said a word since he entered her apartment.

Every touch of his lips had her wondering how kissing such a bad man could feel so good. She could taste herself on him, and he was invading her senses along with her personal space. He was sitting under her hips and between her legs. Adrian was all over her, and she could feel his hard length pushing up against her throbbing sex.

He stopped only long enough to roll on a condom, and Hana put her arms around his neck. She was holding onto him as he pressed himself further into her entrance. With one thrust of his hips, he was inside of her. She was still riding the pulse of her orgasm, and it made her clench around his hard member. She wrapped her legs around him and held on, agreeing again to be a willing participant in his wicked game. She let out a breath of release as he seated himself fully. He was so hard, but she was so wet he slid right in.

Then out. The rhythm intensified as she held onto him. She was riding him again as he feverishly fucked her. She let herself feel the pleasure of having a man between her legs and the way the pleasure came so easily in his arms.

There was no romance, only passion, but it was overwhelming, and he was holding onto her too. Adrian looked into her eyes and in this moment, she swore this was real. His enchanting green eyes lulling her into the fantasy of intimacy.

***

Adrian held onto Hana as she bounced on top of his thighs. He couldn't get enough of her. He couldn't think of a hotter moment in his life than when she was letting him pleasure her, which turned him on even more. He was so hard it was painful, and every time he drove home, he swore he touched heaven.

He was ashamed to say that this was the first time he had ever cared whether the woman had come first. He wanted Hana to find her release. It drove him crazy when he felt her inner walls clench around him, knowing she was going to orgasm. He wanted her more than the first time he had her, and more when she was taking all of him and sitting astride him. He was going to find himself unmanned quickly if she kept moving like that.

It was the way she kept looking at him with those big brown eyes of hers, she and he at the exact same pace. The fire was building up inside her again. She kissed him, and it almost felt like what he imagined love felt like. He knew he didn't love her, but there was something so sweet about her kiss. It was the way she didn't have the capacity to give anything less than everything.

It was why she was worth ten million dollars. More, if she had asked. He had his release ripped from his body without warning. As they stilled, his mouth was still connected to her lips.

It was an intimate moment, and he pulled back a little.

He felt warm but tried to act more composed than he felt. Hana was his drug. He couldn't get away from her. He couldn't even wait in the damn car for her. He was insatiable when it came to her.

He wished he could satisfy this itch he had for her. His hand twitched as she lay back on her bed. He pulled on his pants and walked out of the bedroom into the bathroom.

Hana was the most fascinating creature on the planet, and he was frustrated with how many hours he spent thinking about her. But every time he had her, he wanted her more.

He cleaned himself, avoiding his image in the mirror and the thoughts that were building. He didn't understand why he never felt like he had had enough of her. He wanted her again even now. He went back to the bed and lay down next to her.

She looked over at him. Her hair was falling over her doe brown eyes. He fought the urge to push the hair back from her face. She looked so well loved with her wild hair and her languid pose. Well loved by him.

She was wearing a colorful robe, and he wondered if she had sewn it herself, and if not, where she'd gotten it. He wondered what it would be like to travel the world with her and see it the way she did. She was this colorful thing, this fragile thing. He felt a nagging guilt that he was ruining her.

In some ways he knew he could never buy all of her, and maybe he shouldn't've tried. He replayed the night over in his head. Her opening the door to her apartment and looking like temptation incarnate. Kissing her felt like it was the end of the world. He barely knew her. He didn't have time for this obsession.

"I'm going to Miami for a couple of days," he declared coolly.

He pulled on one of her frilly quilts to cover himself. She was toying with her hair with one hand and petting a cat. He hadn't realized she had one of those.

"I'll be here," she said and smiled.

She always did that, made fun of him. He could tell she knew he didn't like her cat. He ignored the animal as it approached, sniffing him gingerly. She looked at him, still smiling, but this time at their introduction.

"His name is Pumpkin."

He ignored the little orange thing and looked at Hana. He didn't like cats.

He asked, "Can I call you when I come back?"

She looked at him and blinked. He never knew what she was thinking until she was telling him, which was often so he rarely had to guess. He appreciated the frank honesty and kept himself honest with her. They were business partners in a sense.

She nodded but said nothing.

They were silent for a couple of minutes and she kissed him after their brief silence. The kiss was soft and gentle, and he hadn't expected it. There was no passion in the kiss. It didn't lead to them resuming where'd they left off, it was little more than a quick chaste press of Hana's lips on his.

Not particularly memorable.
He thought about it for hours after he left.

Chapter Twelve

Hana didn't hear much from Adrian during the rest of the week. She assumed he was in Miami, or wherever his rich-boy heart decided he needed to be. She took the time to plan a trip across the globe to Central America for Esperanza, to choose sites to build schools while he did who knew what in Florida. He texted her on Friday that he wanted to send a car to pick her up on Saturday. While eating lunch at her desk, she thought about whether she was going to make herself available.

Adrian always gave her the opportunity to say she was busy. Then again, he was liable to show up at her apartment to test her. She didn't know if she wanted to keep this deal going. She considered giving back the money and telling him to go to hell. She wanted to have faith other donors would come along, but to chance that they wouldn't would crush Esperanza, and she wouldn't ever let that happen again.

She wondered if she was suffering from a version of Stockholm syndrome while admitting to herself she wanted him to pick her up on Saturday. Hana considered her sanity as she and Taron decided where to build their next school, and discussed the logistics and availability of contractors to complete the project.

She wondered if she'd tell Adrian about these kinds of decisions. The cold truth was his money had cleared her account and already paid for the trip she was planning. She had kept a part of the money. She'd taken one million, but she still had access to the other nine. She didn't want to ever use the rest of the money, but the truth was Esperanza wasn't getting any more donations anytime soon. For now, the public had turned on them after what had happened. It would take years to win back the good will Bianca took with her when she ran off with Esperanza's money.

People sympathized with her, but all the trust was gone. Until it came back, Hana feared Adrian's money was the only salvation Esperanza had.

She and Taron booked their flights and hired contractors. Hana knew there was no going back from where she found herself. She had sold her body to him, and justified it by telling herself she was doing for Esperanza.

That made it feel like a forever decision. Clearly, taking Adrian's money was something she could never undo. No matter how tempted she was by the passion in his kiss, those nights were bought, and they'd both paid the price. She kept thinking about when she decided to kiss him that last time. The way it felt. Even though they were imitating love, it still resonated in her memory.

She didn't love Adrian, but she felt like she didn't want to turn him down. She wanted to see him for some strange reason. She couldn't describe the madness of it, so, she texted him a yes when her every instinct told her to say no.

On Saturday the sight of Louis in front of her apartment holding open the car door made her laugh. She knew how she got here, but the ridiculousness of the situation hit her. She was a naive fool, and Adrian was an experienced player—fascinating and remote.

Most of the time he was annoying the hell out of her, and the other times he was kissing her senseless. Still, she was surprised to find herself anticipating seeing him.

He wasn't her boyfriend. They weren't in a relationship, but they'd spent two passionate nights together. She knew tonight wouldn't be different. As she knocked on his door, she waited patiently and wondered how many women had stood in the same place before her.

Adrian opened the door, and his green eyes lit up wickedly as he saw her. He looked as annoyingly perfect as the last time she saw him. He yanked her inside by her arm, and Hana found herself hitting him like a wave pitched against the beach. Except the sand was a hard, hot wall of man and muscle colliding into her.

Adrian sealed his lips over hers in a possessive kiss, and Hana shamelessly responded. She kissed him like they were reuniting. Like their new, passionate romance had gotten interrupted by a business trip, and they'd missed each other miserably. Their clench didn't feel like the fraud this affair really was.

Even if it was fraudulent, his kiss still felt like fire on her lips.

Adrian hugged her to him, and for a moment Hana savored the feeling of being enveloped in his arms. She willed the racing of her heart to slow as she pulled away from him. She caught her breath and disentangled herself from the cage of his muscled biceps.

Hana didn't want to desire him like this. She wanted to run, but she couldn't deny the electrifying connection between them. She walked over to his floor-to-ceiling window and quietly touched her fingers to the glass. She knew she was smudging it, but she didn't care if she left a mark on his perfect little world.

Then Adrian was right behind her. He put his hand on top of hers, his large palm enveloping hers completely. She turned around and was met with passion. Adrian had missed her, and he showed her by the way he captured her mouth in a kiss. His tongue claimed hers as he put both of his hands on her hips and pulled them back from the window. They fell onto the couch in a tangle of limbs. Hana ran her fingers through his blond hair and tugged at his head.

Adrian flipped her to straddle him like she weighed nothing. Her hips settled over his, and his right hand splayed against her backside. He used his other hand to flirt with the curve of her waist. Hana arched under his gaze and his touch. There were places on her body that practically ached for his attention.

She moaned as he grasped the fabric of her shirt pulled gently with both hands at the buttons until it opened to reveal her breasts. Hana felt her body heating up in anticipation of his touch, but Adrian took his time to look, feasting on her lacy confection of a bra. His eyes darkened, foreshadowing what he would do with his hands, then placed a finger on her chest and trailed it over the exposed skin above her bra cup.

Hana leaned her head back in surrender.

He shocked her when he said, "I missed these."

Hana burst into laughter. Here he was completely clothed and talking to her breasts.

Adrian chuckled too and kissed the delicate skin over her collarbones. She stopped laughing, cupped the back of his head, and pulled him to her chest. She craved his mouth on her body, and he didn't disappoint. Adrian worshipped her.

***

The sound of the door latch clicking open was jarring. Adrian was distracted by the hellion on his lap when he heard the door opening in the distance. He turned his head as he heard it swing to, and saw his sister walking into the living room. Adrian pulled Hana into his arms and hugged her to his chest. Her shirt was completely open when Lisa walked through the door, and he didn't want Hana to be exposed.

"We need a moment," he called, startling his little sister.

He could tell by the way she slapped her hand against her mouth and said, "Oh my God," that she was shocked. She turned away as Hana buttoned up her shirt.

Adrian was going to kill Lisa.

After a few moments, Lisa turned back toward them. "I am so sorry. I came to borrow one of your cars for the weekend. I thought you were still in Miami." Hana sat back and next to him watching the exchange. He had never intended for her to meet his family, much less wanted to explain who she was to his sister.

His eyes flashed guiltily to Hana. "I came back early," he admitted. He'd been going mad in Miami without Hana. The memory of her hadn't sustained him. He wanted her back in his arms.

Lisa looked at Hana. "My name is Lisa," she said with a smile. "Who are you?"

Adrian didn't let Hana answer. He replied quickly, "Get out, Lisa."

***

While Hana took a moment to ponder whether Adrian left Miami for her, she dismissed the notion as quickly as it came up, especially since it was obvious he was trying to get rid of his sister. Clearly, he didn't want his family to know about Hana, and wasn't that a lovely thought?

Lisa stood there with a determined expression, her arms crossed over her chest. Adrian sighed, then said quickly, "Lisa, this is Hana. Hana, this is my sister." He stared at Lisa, then instructed, "Now please leave my apartment. No, you may not borrow my car. You have enough money to buy your own. Wreck your own cars, Lisa, and get out."

She ignored him and continued talking to Hana. “Are you his girlfriend?” Hana looked over at him, and he gave her nothing. As always. The hell with it. She decided to lie.

“Yes,” she said quickly, because she didn’t like the truth and she felt foolish sitting in his apartment after being caught with her shirt open and him enjoying her breasts.

He looked over at her and gave her an odd look, indicating he didn’t think they were in a relationship. At this point, she didn’t really care. She was going to save face, and he’d have to deal with it. Hana hadn’t been ready to meet Adrian’s sister, who was intimidating like her brother, but Hana didn’t back down from Lisa’s steady gaze as she inspected Hana.

Lisa tilted her head and said “I’ve never met a girlfriend before,” then considered Hana with an appraising glance. “Come to think of it, I’ve never seen anyone at Adrian’s apartment. Are you coming to dinner too?” she asked quickly, the presumption clearly being made was evident by her changing facial expressions. Both of the women looked at Adrian.

He answered for Hana again, which she didn’t appreciated. “I wasn’t planning to go at all. I’m engaged this evening.”

Lisa looked positively gleeful. “I’ll tell everyone you’re engaged if you don’t let me borrow your car.”

“Blackmail?” he asked pursing his lips. He looked so funny sitting there, crossing his legs in his suit and arguing with his sister. In a stern tone he said, “We’re not engaged.”

Lisa turned to Hana. “You should come to dinner, if you want to, Hana. My mother and I would love that. Even our dad would love to meet,” she lifted her chin in Adrian’s direction, “his girlfriend. I’m going to tell everyone how beautiful you are. Though, I question your taste in men.”

Hana smiled. “Maybe,” she responded diplomatically. “Regardless, it was nice to meet you, Lisa.” His sister was taunting Adrian, and Hana didn’t feel sorry for him. He’d have to figure his own way out of this. Hana found it hard to sympathize with him. He came up with their “agreement.” It was his to explain. She didn’t know whether there was an NDA in their contract, but she wouldn’t be the one to tell people about their arrangement.

He ground out the words, a crack in his usually calm demeanor. “I’m coming to dinner.”

"Fine," Lisa said smugly and Hana had to admire the young woman. She knew Adrian's weaknesses and played them like a pro. She'd convinced him to attend a dinner he clearly didn't want to attend. In that moment, Hana realized her man of stone had a soft spot for family. It was easy to see he wanted to please his sister.

"Please get out," he repeated for the third time.

"Why?" Lisa said and put her hand on her hips. She had the same stubborn look on her face Hana had seen on Adrian's too often, and Lisa had the same bright blond hair and striking green eyes. The familial resemblance was obvious even in soft lighting. Lisa was tall and slender and seemed to have the same arrogant *I do what I want* attitude her brother had.

"My girlfriend and I are going to have sex now." She didn't know what was more shocking the fact that he called her his girlfriend or that he announced his plans for the evening. She figured it was him calling her his girlfriend because it sounded so dirty coming from his lips. They didn't act like boyfriend and girlfriend, only in the bedroom. She flushed in response. The familial encounter seemed to stretch on for an eternity.

Lisa groaned and covered her ears. "Oh my god. I don't want to hear this." She went to the bowl on the table where there was a pile of keys.

He looked at Hana as he said to Lisa, "Leave your key to the apartment." He looked like a promise unfulfilled again, and she hated that he had that effect on her.

"That's my sister," he whispered after Lisa took a set of keys, didn't leave her apartment key, smirked, and then left.

"I see that," Hana whispered back. "She's a lovely girl."

"She's nosy," he stated with annoyance.

"She cares about you," Hana told him the obvious. "You've never introduced a girlfriend to your family before?"

It was weird, but the look that passed over his face said he hadn't. "I have," he insisted. "But it's been a while."

Chapter Thirteen

Hana was completely unconvinced by Adrian's act. There was something to the higher pitched voice and something about the words *But it's been a while* that made her doubt him. There was also the way Lisa spoke that made Hana think he never had a girlfriend. She studied his profile. His perpetually groomed, gold yellow hair was fanned to the side and his jaw was set in a hard line. Those irreverent green eyes were staring back at her with an annoyed set to his full pink lips. He definitely didn't want to talk about girlfriends right now.

Adrian was a gorgeous billionaire playboy, which meant it wasn't outside the realm of possibility that he had never had a girlfriend who lasted long enough to meet the sister. He might be the type of man who only trifled with women. Hana had to remind herself not to look for promises of affection and long-term planning, regardless of how charming he could be when he wanted. What they had was a wanton sexual affair not a love match.

Adrian was elegantly dressed as ever, his bright blue suit folded as he crossed his legs and considered her. Even at home, he dressed as if he was heading to the office. He'd returned from the airport, showered, shaved, and then dressed to kill. She could smell the cologne of his aftershave. Had she been home, Hana would've changed into her robe by now and collapsed on the couch. Adrian looked like he was ready to entertain guests.

Hana turned her head. She had never seen the opulently white apartment in daylight. Everything she and Adrian did was in the dark of night, secretive and sinful. She didn't recognize the methodically designed place. The room was bright with natural light from the sun. The city's skyline looked calmer in the gray fog of day. She took in his sparse décor. Wooden bowls on his mahogany coffee table and succulents in hanging pots coming down from the ceiling.

It would have made an excellent Architectural Digest feature. She always wondered what type of people lived in neutered uncluttered places like this. Cold-hearted, girlfriendless Adrian Douglas lived here. They were still sitting on his pristine white couches, and he was folding his arms over his chest, signaling he had every intention of avoiding conversation. It was also completely possible that Adrian didn't want to talk to Hana in particular. They weren't in a relationship, and this wasn't the third date where they shared about past relationships.

"How long has it been?" she asked, refusing to let the subject drop. He didn't get to decide when they stopped talking. She had a lot of questions about him. She knew absolutely nothing about this man other than his net worth. The secrecy stopped now.

He flicked a brow up. "Can't remember," he said off-handedly. He was unreadable, staring at her and deflecting a true answer.

For some reason, she needed to draw him out. She knew his past shouldn't matter, but she wanted him to talk to her. There had to be more to him than tons of money and hot sex. She figured, she'd break the ice and maybe that would help him loosen up. "I broke up with my boyfriend last year," she said quietly. "We were together for three years."

When he didn't say anything or comment, she questioned why she was telling him about herself. He didn't care about her. Adrian didn't even like her. He always froze when she tried to get to know him. He only knew how to seduce and fuck. Clearly, he didn't want the girlfriend experience. He'd bought and paid for her, and she wondered if she was the first or another in a long string of many.

"I've never had a girlfriend." He shrugged and said evenly, "My dates tend to be one night only affairs."

She was stunned. Adrian had never had a girlfriend, which meant he had never been in love. Though, it made sense. Nothing about their "arrangement" was normal. She felt sorry for him. Even if he got some pleasure from sleeping with women only once or twice, he had never experienced true intimacy. There was something special about a relationship that weathered the passage of time where each person knew the other better with each passing day. It made the love sweeter over time.

This ruthlessly beautiful man was affluent and powerful. Women would want to be with him regardless whether he was offering love or passion. But why pay for it? She knew at least ten women who would throw themselves at him because of the way he looked. Others would have sex with him because he was wealthy hoping for some designer compensation. Or, if they were really ambitious, an apartment.

A man like Adrian could definitely get women without a contract, which made Hana wonder again about the commitment she had signed. Nothing about his tastes in the bedroom struck her as kinky. The way he had sex made her think he was vulnerable in some ways. Sometimes he kissed quite sweetly. All that money and privilege, and she pitied him. He had never had someone love him without being compensated for acting like it.

She asked, "So, you bring them back to your house and you give them money?"

He leaned back and cocked his head. "No," he said indignantly as if he hadn't propositioned her. "I've never given any woman money before."

She found herself rearing back in surprise. "Excuse me?"

He shook his head. "I've never paid anyone to have sex with me." Flippantly, he clarified, "I've never had to pay any time I've ever wanted a woman."

She figured women threw themselves at his feet. So why pay her? If he'd applied more of his charm and less of his business skills, he probably could've convinced her to accept his dinner invitation the night of the gala. She probably wouldn't have slept with him on the first date, though who knows. He could be charming and convincing with only a little effort. Even now she wanted to kiss him and be in his arms again. He didn't have to throw ten million dollars in her face to get her to sleep with him. He only had to put in a minor bit of wooing. Maybe he didn't know how. It was like he didn't know how to make a real connection with a woman. More likely, he didn't care to try.

"You paid me," she stated. "Why?"

She knew her worth, and it had nothing to do with money. He had put a price on her. Ten million reasons why she would never understand him.

He uncrossed his arms and leaned forward a bit. "I don't know," he said. "I think I knew the only way to have you was through your charity, and I wanted to have you." His eyes darkened. "At any cost.

The more I've been around you, the more I can't seem to stop wanting to see you. I wish you'd said yes to me that night, when I asked you to dinner."

"Don't put your choice to 'buy' me on me," she snapped.

***

She was right. The crumbling civility and unease between them was Adrian's fault. She was allowed to turn him down. He should've tried harder. He should've waited for her permission. But he wanted her then, and he wanted her more now. He found himself impatient to be around her. In Miami, he felt the loss of her presence keenly.

He'd missed her more than he cared to admit, and seeing her handle Lisa's presumptuous cross-examination so well, had his emotions plunged into chaos. He couldn't stop the twinge of excitement when she'd declared herself his girlfriend. It was an odd sensation, worrying but not without its benefits. He'd enjoyed the sound of the word on her lips. He'd relished the look of her freshly kissed and disheveled on his couch. He'd wanted Lisa to leave because he wanted to continue what he and Hana had started.

She was sitting on his couch in her jeans and denim blouse. He would've had both of those things off of her in a matter of moments at the rate they were going if Lisa hadn't showed up.

Hana's hair was still tousled in a curly ruckus around her shoulders, and her blouse was hastily buttoned to her sternum. He could still see the appealing curves of her breasts in the vee of her shirt and wanted to resume their interrupted interlude.

But she was giving him the third degree, and somehow he admitted to never having had a girlfriend. There was something about her he couldn't put his finger on. He'd never spent so much of his time thinking about a woman like he thought about her. He'd never even had the urge to take a woman to dinner. He found himself stalking her office at the late hours, begging her to leave so he could tempt her into his bedroom.

He went to Miami to look at property, but found himself wondering how long he could stand to be away from her. This obsession with her was bad for business. She was bewitchingly elusive, requiring more time, effort, and candor than he had ever given a woman. He found it easier to offer her money than submit to her questions.

Questions brought answers, and he wasn't ready to share everything about himself. That he answered at all demonstrated how differently he was treating her compared to all the other women he'd bedded.

He was courting Hana, in his own sadistic way. He had never dated a woman, and this was him trying to do it. He had never wanted to spend time with a woman. And he certainly never wanted to find out what motivated her as much as he did Hana. He wanted to be with her all the time.

He knew he was the worst kind of man. Not only because he made her sign a contract, but because of how he had treated women before. Rarely had he spent a full night with most women. Now he saw that they required care, time, and honest questions and uncomfortable truths. Hana was asking all of that from him and he didn't know if he could give it to her. He certainly hadn't given a woman so much before.

He had never felt more naked than he did right now, and he was still wearing one of his sharkskin suits.

"Don't break the contract," he replied to her stinging rebuke. "You agreed to one year." He didn't know how to woo a woman like Hana, but he had bought himself a year to figure it out. Or figure out how to get her out of his system.

"I know that," she hissed. She was angry with him, but he didn't care. Ten million dollars. For three hundred and sixty-five of her days. He told himself he'd grow tired of her before the year was over. He'd promised himself he'd be back to business before the month was out.

He had to be callous, or he wouldn't survive this insanity. This wanting her.

***

Hana was tired of trying to understand him, and she wondered why she bothered. He didn't care about her, and she decided to return the favor. She'd offer him what he'd paid for.

"Do you want me to take off my clothes?" she asked. The way she said it made him release a deep and measured breath in response.

For the first time she wasn't as eager as she'd been in their past encounter. She didn't care if he wanted her to stay or go. Staying in this complicated black hole of emotions with Adrian made her feel lost. At least if she left, she'd have some quiet time by herself, and she'd push him out of her mind.

"I want you to come to dinner with me," he stated, clearly having made a decision he chose not to share. He was looking at her directly in the eyes. She was trying to read his expression. "You're quite beautiful even when you're angry," he said charmingly. "As you should be. I'm sorry," he finished softly.

"Is that part of the contract?" she asked, tipping her chin up and setting her shoulders back. She felt defiant and would continue to defy him at every turn. He still hadn't explained why she had been chosen to sign the contract. She wondered why he would want to have dinner with her at all. He could continue to sweep her under the carpet and leave whatever they had out of the cold light of day.

"No," he admitted, looking at the view through the floor-to-ceiling glass wall. Vulnerable Adrian was back, and Hana didn't understand how he turned his emotions on and off. "I'm asking you if you're interested in having dinner with my family. It'll be us, Lisa, and our parents." He didn't offer any other details, and since she couldn't wrap her mind around why he was asking, she didn't need further clarification.

"I see." Of one thing she was certain: he was hoping she'd say yes. She knew it in her bones, as if he had his hand out for her to take. It was like a dance with him. Sometimes the exciting parts distracted her, but she knew after the desire died down to an ember, there was this.

Adrian stared into her eyes and invited her to stare into his. To take his hand, and be with him. She sensed he'd never been down this path and what they were to each other was a mystery. Nonetheless, she reacted as she always did, she trusted her instincts.

"Yes," she said quietly. "I'll go to dinner with you, Adrian."

***

When Lisa had walked through the door, Adrian had hugged Hana to his chest and had hidden her from view. Every time she kissed him, he forgot everything else going on in the world. He had actually flown back two days early because he missed her that damn badly. He didn't say it in so many words, but when he pulled her through the door, he felt his heart flip when he saw her.

Then she was in his arms and kissing him senseless. His Hana, with her big brown eyes and her kissable mouth that she used to put him in his place. He wanted her to do that now. Put him in his place, but stay here with him. Lisa had interrupted what he had planned to be a pleasure filled evening. Every night he'd been in Miami, he'd been thinking up ways to have her claw off his clothes. Now that he had her in his arms, it was hard to let her go.

Then she went and called herself his girlfriend, and he found himself wishing it was true. He wished his sister had walked in on them after he'd sated his desire for Hana. She wasn't his girlfriend, only his for the night, and he reminded himself this wasn't a real relationship. It was an experiment to see how long this craving would continue. But when his sister had also asked her to join them for dinner and Hana had told her maybe, a part of him began to wish she was considering attending. There was a certain level of familiarity he wished to have with Hana. A natural closeness he'd shut off when he'd drawn up that contract.

He wished that a woman like Hana was with him. Not because she felt obligated to or was paid to. Adrian wanted a version of Hana who wasn't here in his home only to take off her clothes, but who had decided she wanted to stay with him.

He liked her near.

He wanted her in a way that defied logic.

He wanted her with him at his family's house.

Nothing could have surprised him more than when she'd said yes.

Chapter Fourteen

They agreed to get her a change of clothing. She had consented to be his date with composure, but inside Hana was terrified. This wasn't part of the deal. These emotions were exhausting. She felt conflicted. Part of her wanted Adrian in a way that was purely sexual, but part of her wanted more from him. She wanted to get to know him, understand how his mind worked, and maybe even ask him how his day was. That feeling was alarming in the context of the money that had been exchanged and the deal they'd made.

It was easy to admit to herself she had missed Adrian when he was gone. His presence and the sheer attraction she felt for him hadn't abated. She had also missed his brooding face, and she had gotten used to experiencing life the Adrian way.

She looked over at him again in the backseat of his car while Louis drove them. She was wearing one of her better white dinner dresses that accentuated what she considered to be her best feature, her curves. Adrian had remained pristine and untouched from their encounter on the couch and was wearing his immaculately cut, azure blue suit.

Given their "agreement," she found it odd to be going on a "meet the parents" dinner date. Even if there was no contract between them, the relationship would be moving too fast. She wasn't ready to get acquainted with his parents. If they'd been on a "normal" relationship path, they'd still be in the *getting to know you* phase, trying to determine if they liked each other enough to *meet the parents*. Having dinner with his family knowing Adrian paid to have sex with her, and that he'd never done that before...there was nothing about tonight that was appealing.

Regardless of the weirdness, she had to make a good impression. She'd put on her nude stilettoes, smoked up her eyes, and pinned a section of her hair back from her face with an unusual multi-colored beaded pin she got in Accra where she'd built a couple of small schools. One of the many places she'd remember for the rest of her life. She'd been across the globe many times, but she never felt more like she was in foreign territory than she did now with Adrian.

He would never be the man for her, no matter how much she fantasized he could be. He'd never had a girlfriend, gave her ten million dollars to make her his for a year, and possessed her body like he was in love with her.

But he wasn't in love with her, and he could turn on a dime. To trust Adrian was to trust the ocean not to make waves, and for the moon not to rise. She'd be waiting an eternity. She couldn't turn a toad into a prince, even though Adrian gave a good impersonation of one.

Hana had to laugh when Louis turned down Lombard Street. Of course his parents lived on San Francisco's most infamous block. The car paused on the road as the vehicle sized iron gate opened on a driveway to a home four times the size of a typical row house.

This was one of those moments where she acknowledged how different Adrian's and her upbringings were. She'd lived in this city all her life and never seen a driveway like this. She couldn't imagine Adrian's hand-stitched loafers ever stepping in her childhood neighborhood.

It was like they grew up in two different cities. She knew Adrian earned his own money and worked more hours than she did, but she had to wonder how successful she would have been, or anyone else she knew for that matter, if they'd grown up in a house like this.

She pulled on the handle and opened the door for herself as Adrian met her on her side of the car. She took his hand as he helped her exit, and Louis drove away at the same time Adrian turned her toward the house.

A man she figured must be Henry Douglas opened the door as Adrian walked her up to the steps of the inclined entrance to the house. She took a deep inhale as if she were on the precipice about to fall, and Adrian put a hand on her lower back.

It was an intimate and comforting touch, but a little disconcerting. He looked down at her and kissed her cheek softly. It wasn't the kind of kiss that blew her mind or made her melt, it was tender and thoughtful. Like he wanted to reassure her that he cared about her.

Except that was a lie. They didn't talk about what they'd say to his family. They were playing a game where Hana was pretending to be his girlfriend, and only she knew she didn't want to play.

Yet... She liked the feeling of his hand on her back as he led her up the stairs. On the car ride over, Adrian had told her stories of Lisa and him terrorizing each other night and day while his father tried to keep the peace. His mother was a quiet elegant soul who'd rather watch the chaos work itself out while having a cup of tea. From the little he'd shared, his family sounded lovely. If he hadn't given her ten million dollars to have sex, maybe she could've been excited to be here. Instead as she looked up at Henry, she was terrified.

Adrian was the spitting image of his father and looking at Henry Douglas was jarring. It was like a preview of what Adrian would look like in thirty years, practically unchanged. He had the same flaxen blond hair, but with a beard speckled with silver. His face was more mature and he had attractive laugh lines, but the eyes were the same, as were the dramatic cheekbones.

It was a shame, she thought, that men like Adrian would change so little over the years. Every year Adrian lived a life of excess and hedonism, his face should show the ravage. Instead she noticed the same sparkle in his father's green eyes that Adrian had. It was hard to look at the pair of them. Nearly mirror images standing next to each other.

Henry was flawlessly attired in a slim fit herringbone suit with a sweater layered over his button-down. His white sneakers were playfully youthful and his smile aimed at her seemed genuine. He hugged her quickly and welcomed her into his home. Hana tried not to hold his wealth against him. She felt like she was well on her way to cynical and mistrusting and needed to remind herself to think twice and speak once, if at all.

As they came into the entryway, she could see that the home was stunning.

The vestibule led to a large open space, which connected the kitchen. Wall to wall clean wood lines and immaculately white quartz countertops highlighted the bright ivory family room with gargantuan off-white linen couches. There was an alabaster sitting area with gold and green accent pillows to the side of the family room. A reading area of sorts. The side room was double the size of her apartment.

Henry led them past the family room through sliding glass doors to the outdoors, crossing under a pergola with crystal chandeliers. A lovely middle-aged woman Hana guessed was Adrian's mother walked up the stone steps from the garden and greeted Hana with a hug and a glass of red wine. Rebecca Douglas was serenely dignified in her collared blue shirt dress, which brushed the tops of her calves.

She wore a necklace of small pink pearls and her bright blonde hair was swept into a neat knot at the nape of her neck. She sipped her wine and introduced herself. Her brown eyes seemed sensitive and warm.

In another world Hana could've enjoyed meeting these people. She felt the generosity in them and wondered how Adrian turned out the way he did. She wondered how he felt about her being here and if he would regret inviting her to meet his parents.

Rebecca led Hana out to the terraced garden and invited her to sit on the enormous U-shaped couch. Rebecca sat on one side, and Hana joined her. The furniture was oversized and so comfortable, Hana sunk into the cushions.

The U-shaped sofa surrounded a fire pit. Soft flames rose up from smooth stones on a rectangular stand. Rebecca was effortlessly beautiful, and Hana noticed she was barefoot when she kicked her feet under her and settled on the couch.

Everyone else was wearing their shoes. Adrian certainly hadn't kicked off his. Hana tried to relax while sitting on the couch with Adrian and his parents. Their outdoor hilltop space was lit by the setting sun streaming over the city skyline. She was starting to feel comfortable until Rebecca asked her how they met.

Hana eyed Adrian who sat stone-faced. Seeing he'd be no help, she told the truth. "At a gala for my charity."

***

It was the kind of question Adrian hadn't thought they'd have to field when he invited her. Actually, he didn't think period. He wasn't prone to impulsive gestures, but he'd wanted Hana to come to his parent's house for dinner, and now he was considering why.

He wanted Hana to be his girlfriend. When they were on their way over, he realized she was the perfect woman. She was unbelievably smart, she had a great sense of humor, and she was endlessly good-natured. It didn't hurt that she was the prettiest woman he'd ever seen. She looked like a snack in that pearly white dress. He liked the way her hair looked too, pinned off her face, the curls rolling down her back. Her brown eyes practically glowed and her cheeks were pink from sitting outdoors.

As they'd walked up to the house he decided he had to figure out a way to convince her to be his for real. He wanted her to give him a chance.

Then there was his family. He'd seen the gleam in his mother's eyes when she hugged Hana, and his dad had been a little too eager when he'd opened the door. Adrian wanted to let them have their moment. He was the kind of man who had never said the word girlfriend when referring to himself. His parents were normal. Social. They liked to fantasize he'd settle down and meet a nice girl.

Hana, was one of the nicest he'd ever met. She wore her heart on her sleeve and everyone could see she was a good person. He'd never spent more time smiling then when he was with her. She had a way about her that made it seem like he had always known her, yet she didn't let him get away with anything.

His parents were sitting across from them, and Adrian smiled inwardly. They were enjoying Hana's company. She was describing her charity and how she and Taron started it. Lisa came out of the house and joined them at the oversized seating area.

Now was his favorite time of day. Twilight was nearly upon them, and the orange and red sunset painted the skyscrapers. He found himself staring at Hana as she looked at the view. He realized he could really grow to care about her.

Hana looked over at him before answering, and she told them about the gala.

He didn't know if what he was feeling was falling in love, since he'd never experienced it before, but the sensation made him feel like he was going to be sick. Then he thought about how she saw him. The bad guy. An evil man wielding his money and power.

There'd be no reason for her to ever fall in love with him.

Chapter Fifteen

When Hana had appeared at the top of the stairs, Adrian had been entranced. She was a vision. A siren, calling him to her. He couldn't wait to get her to dance. To have her in his arms. His reverie was broken when his sister laughed at how they met.

"My brother actually attended one of those?"

"I do from time to time," he defended himself. "I support many charities." He looked into Hana's eyes. Hers was the only charity he had personally ensured would survive. He didn't fully understand what made Hana so different and why he hadn't pursued her the way other men would have. If he'd done what was considered "normal," they'd probably be here having dinner with his parents, and she'd be happy. Maybe even enchanted with him.

Adrian knew if there was a hell, he'd probably end up there while Hana would be on her perch somewhere in heaven.

"Well, I had just completed my speech," she directly at him as she spoke, "and Adrian came up to me and asked me to dance." It sounded like a pretty story when she said it like that.

Rebecca smiled. "Well done, Adrian." If they believed only what Hana told them, he came off sounding like the perfect gentleman. The truth was no fairy tale, and was way less than honorable.

Lisa exclaimed, "I've never seen my brother dance."

Adrian could remember clearly every moment of their dance. How Hana looked in that haunting black dress as they whirled around the dance floor. His motives had been entirely self-indulgent. He wanted to be with the most exquisite woman in the room. He wanted to get to know her. He still did. He didn't know if he had any goodness to offer her, and after cornering her into their contract, he was sure she wouldn't think so. Her worth was more than money could buy.

“I had seen her from across the room, and I had to talk to her,” he said. Actually, he’d been compelled. Drawn to her inexplicably. “I asked her out, and she immediately turned me down.”

Everyone laughed, even him. Though, now looking back, he didn’t respect her wishes in the matter at all, and was sorry he hadn’t.

“And then...” she said trailing off. She held her hand out for him to continue. She was daring him to tell the lie his parents needed to hear.

After forcing her into a devil’s bargain, he could see in his mind’s eye the way he made her strip down and get into his bed. She had taken off her clothes. The memory of it, and her was on his mind every waking hour of every day.

Rendered stupid, and unable to come up with a plausible lie, he didn’t respond, and she continued for him. “Then we decided I was wrong. I should’ve gone to dinner with him.”

He smiled faintly at her with acid burning under his tongue. He liked that made-up part of their story. The idea that they would have gotten to be together on their own, at a slower pace, the way other couples did. But they didn’t have that history. She signed her name on his contract, and forfeited her free will for her charity.

If he closed his eyes, he could pretend this was another quiet evening with his family, but this time with Hana in the picture, fitting in well. He hoped he could convince her she belonged with him. He wasn’t noble or experienced in being a good guy, but he could learn to be.

He would try for her.

Hana’s eyes lit up as she spoke of Esperanza. She was head over heels in love with what she did, and it was one of the many reasons she compelled him.

She turned to his father and said, “We’re headed to Guatemala next month and we’re going to build five schools.”

“That’s amazing,” his mother remarked. “I love your mission, it’s truly motivating. We heard on the news you’ve had donations come in after that...unpleasantness. We’re happy Esperanza’s back on its feet.”

Adrian turned to Hana reeling from the news she’d be going away. From him. She’d be thousands of miles away, wrapped up in her charity work, doing what she loved. He wanted to demand she tell him about things like this. Clearly, she had been planning this since she got the money. Why did she have leave him?

"We're happy too." Hana shot Adrian a sidelong glance. "Esperanza works with local partners to build the schools," she told them. "It's twelve grueling weeks, but it's really rewarding."

"Twelve weeks?" He wanted to be sure he heard her correctly.

"Yes." She seemed way too happy about this. "We're leaving in less than a month so we're scrambling to get everything in place."

Scrambling to not tell him. He got her play. This was her way of telling him that he didn't have any say in what she did when it came to her charity. Clever woman outwitted him by letting him know of her plans in front of his family. He couldn't say anything now. But later...

"You oversee all the builds?" Lisa asked.

"I'm not there on every project, but either Taron or I have our eyes on every building that goes up," Hana explained. "We built this company out of her mom's garage. We're all in."

This was the conversation they should've had alone. He couldn't react. Not the way he wanted to. She was going to Guatemala and the message was clear. *Don't try to change her mind.* He might try. He was definitely going to try.

"I'll miss you when you're gone," he said quietly. He picked up her hand and kissed it, then kept it laced with his as he continued to stare at her beautiful profile.

He meant it. His life would be empty without Hana. He couldn't stand being away from her when he was in Miami, and that was only a few days. What was he going to do for three months?

Rebecca and Lisa looked at him with soft expressions, like it was sweet he would miss his new girlfriend. If only they knew how his gut roiled. He hated that anything would take her away from him. He didn't recognize himself, and how violently ill he felt at the thought of her leaving.

Tipping her head, she asked so only he could hear, "What are you looking at?"

"I'm watching you," he whispered. The rays of the sun's last beams were gleaming over her head. He almost laughed. It looked like a halo.

"Watching me while I talk?"

"Yes."

She cocked her head. “Too weird. Focus on something else.”

“As you wish,” he said, but his gaze never wavered from her. There wasn’t anything more visually arresting than the curve of Hana’s cheek as she smiled.

She laughed. “You’re still staring.”

“Can you blame me?” He lifted her fingers again and put them up to his mouth. He held them there for a long moment at his lips.

***

Hana felt like her hand had been burned by this kiss. The intensity she felt rolling off him was visceral, and she wondered what his intentions were. He was always naughty, but sometimes it seemed like he really wanted to be nice. Decent. Those times she veered into crazy-ville for a few minutes thinking maybe he could really be her boyfriend.

Then her sanity returned. He was a bad man and she couldn’t forget it. She couldn’t let kisses on her hand distract her. Not good wine and pretty architecture or a classy family that praised her charity. She needed to have a level head around Adrian. He was manipulative and selfish. If she wanted to survive with her heart intact, she’d have to figure out a way to keep her emotions in check. Adrian was like an ocean. He’d carry her away before she’d realize she was miles from shore.

She had ten million reasons to never trust him.

This man had never had a girlfriend. He couldn’t stomach a commitment. There was no reason to expect she was the exception to the rule. She’d like to see how ardently he missed her after three months of separation. Hana couldn’t see him inspired by her after that long an absence. She didn’t think Adrian had it in him to be faithful.

The rest of the evening went by quickly. His family maintained easy dinner conversation, and made her feel welcome. After dessert, Hana said her thanks and Adrian made their goodbyes.

She knew it’d been sneaky to announce her trip to Central America where he couldn’t protest. The contract said she was supposed to available when he wanted her, but she had a charity to run. That was the purpose of the money. She wasn’t so naïve as to believe she wouldn’t get blistered by his anger on the way home.

When they got in the car, he started in with the questions immediately.

"How long is less than a month?" he ground out. "How long before you go?"

"Thirteen days," she told the window, keeping her head turned away from him. From day one, she'd told him Esperanza was her priority. He knew she took the money for her charity. He couldn't be surprised she meant to use it.

"Sounds dangerous," he said as if he were concerned for her safety. She'd bet he was going to start to try to convince her not to go.

"It's not," she told him.

***

Adrian looked at the determination on her face and decided on another tact. He looked out of his side of the car, watching the shoreline. Night had fallen and in the window's reflection he saw defeat in his expression. This wasn't him. He didn't do defeat.

"I don't know why you do the work yourself, when you could hire people to do it."

Hana shook her head. "You can't buy everything, Adrian," she said with a quiet sadness about her.

She was talking about her work, but she was referring to herself. She looked so proud sitting on the other side of the car with her shoulders set against the world. She really was beautiful. He'd like to think he could say something that would change the essence of their relationship. Stop the clock, turn it back, and make Hana look at him the way she looked at him that night, when he was just a man asking her to dance. But he couldn't think of anything to say that would alter their course.

He could demand she not leave. Enforce the terms of their agreement. Remind her she had to be available to him whenever he wanted her, but where would that get him? She'd despise him more than she did now, and tonight, after playing pretend in front of his family, he didn't have it in him to fight her.

So he took her home.

His for now.

Chapter Sixteen

Hana looked down at her phone. She hadn't heard from Adrian in three days. The words *anytime I want you* took on a whole new light as she looked at the empty inbox. She found it easy to hate him, hate the contract, and hate the money. She knew she was justified. But now as she was sitting in her office looking out her window at an urban garden wondering how many times she'd checked her phone in the last seventy-two hours.

It was the kisses like the one on her hand that had her thinking Adrian was some kind of dark angel, redeemable. But all her good sense said she was insane.

He made her insane. She couldn't deny they had a connection in the bedroom. Or he was really good at making her feel like they did. Maybe he was a good lover and treated everybody like that. She took a beat and imagined Adrian with another woman. It turned out to be a gut-wrenching thought. The fact it tormented her at all was a problem. The thought of Adrian with someone else shouldn't have affected her at all. She kicked herself again and wondered if there was an exclusivity cause in their agreement. These were the unbalanced thoughts of a deranged person or a clingy girlfriend.

She couldn't count on her sanity, and she obviously couldn't count on Adrian. She thought for the millionth time about texting him. But maybe the reason why he didn't contact her was because he didn't want her anymore. Knowing she'd be gone for three months put him off her. She didn't want to examine how that made her feel. She reminded herself Adrian had paid her for a year but had told her many times he didn't expect their liaison to last that long. She questioned what kind of mental illness was affecting her that she would want him to want her again. Hana rubbed her temples. She was starting to get a headache.

"Have you eaten?" he said from out of the darkness, the articulation with autocratic inflection only Adrian could manage.

Even though her eyes were closed, the sound of his voice made her smile.

Of course, he was here. It was like she could conjure him with her mind. As soon as she thought about texting him, he appeared. She opened her eyes and shook her head. Adrian was standing in front of her, leaning against the doorway, taking up the entire frame. He was holding a brown paper bag and she suspected it contained food. He had only a few preoccupations: work, food, and she hoped darkly, her.

He was wearing a navy pinstripe suit that was cut tightly against his lean, muscled body. After he threw his coat on a chair, he sat in front of her desk. His light blond hair was expertly combed to the side, and his green eyes were sparkling. She could tell he enjoyed sneaking up on her. His sensuous mouth was curved into a sinful smirk as he cavalierly stretched out in a seat in front of her.

She was sitting on the other side of her desk, and she put her hands down slowly and placed them in front of her. She touched the tips of her palms together and considered him. "Did you even think to call to let me know you would be stopping by?"

It didn't matter she wanted him here. It didn't matter she'd been spending all her time thinking about him. She had to let him know it wasn't okay to show up whenever the spirit moved him.

"No," he said. He was so big, and the chair was comically small underneath him. He took up the space in every room he was in. He was larger than life.

"Yet," she said, "I have to make an appointment to go to your office."

He crossed his legs. "No, you don't," he stated. "You can come in whenever you like. Louis knows who you are."

"Wait. Louis is your driver, right?" she asked. "Your personal assistant's name is Louis too?"

He nodded.

"There's something weird about that."

"It's a common name." He shrugged. "I'm able to keep them straight. I think you'll manage."

She sighed. He made her head run in circles. The headache was back. "That's not the point."

"I get it. The point is I should have called. I'm sorry. I was a little preoccupied." There it was, another quick smile and easy agreement. When he did that, she knew he was up to something since his smiles were so rare and precious. She wondered what was in the bag. He'd placed it on her desk and hadn't mentioned it.

"That was too easy," Hana said and cleared her throat. "Usually, you're not so agreeable. What do you want?"

His smile disappeared into his signature frown.

"I'm always agreeable," he said, with his high and mighty arrogance. He pushed the bag toward her over her desk.

"It's called a *kouign amann*. Try it."

She didn't argue. She was famished. She was running on a gallon of coffee and not much else. He smiled as she opened the paper bag. She took the laminated pastry out of the bag and held it up to her lips, then took a bite.

"See that was easy."

She closed her eyes and chewed. He was insufferable. Unbelievably handsome, but absolutely unbearable. However, this baked, buttery snack flaked like a croissant and was the most delicious thing she had ever eaten. Hana ignored him and tried to enjoy the treat despite his presence. She tasted the confection's caramel flavor and chewed on the bready little cloud. It was absolutely decadent. She opened her eyes to look at him.

"I was working you know," she said tightly. That was a complete lie. She should have been working, but she was thinking about Adrian.

He nodded and said, "You have to get ready for your trip."

"I do."

Adrian held his hand out for her to give her little treat up to him.

"Get your own."

He tucked a paper napkin above his tie in preparation. He was so prissy sometimes. She handed the delicacy over. Hana watched him take it into his hand and the sugar crystals immediately coated the inside of his palm. He took an eager bite.

"It's heaven," he said, after swallowing.

She couldn't help but laugh. Adrian with a paper napkin stuffed in collar holding a dainty patisserie in his hand. She knew he disliked finger food, and loved using utensils.

"Give it back," she ordered, wiggling her fingers at him. "Your bites are humongous."

He smiled and handed it back, looking at his dirtied hands. She would bet he wanted to run to the restroom and wash them off. Then he met her gaze with a twinkle as he slowly brought his fingers to his lips. He licked the sugar off his index finger and she felt it in her stomach. She shook her head. He was the definition of a bad boy. He was liable to have her bent over a desk if she closed the door. She had to get him out of here.

"I have work to do," she repeated. "How can I help you?"

Adrian took the napkin from his collar and stood up. Hana rose too. She cleaned her hand with a napkin and threw it on her desk. She blinked and he was right in front of her, totally in her space. He was looking at her seriously again, like he had something important to say.

"I won't stay, but I wanted to tell you I've been thinking a lot lately. A lot about you."

That stopped her heart completely. That and his nearness, and his pretty boy face. She was afraid she was falling in love with that face, as crazy as it sounded. She couldn't have stopped him talking for the world.

"I think you're one of the most special people," he started then stopped. "That sounds silly." It didn't sound silly to her.

He tried again. "I like you, Hana." She knew she was in trouble. "I was wondering if you would kiss me."

He was asking for something he'd taken without permission before, and she didn't understand why. The question hung in the air like he wanted her to claim him, her golden fallen angel.

If she did it, she would be agreeing to walk that line with him of bliss and heartbreak, of heights then disaster. She was Icarus, and stupidly she decided to leap.

***

When Adrian walked through the door, he hadn't expected to be caught up by so many emotions. She looked sad and tired. He wondered if he was the one who was making her feel that way. She had tortured his every waking moment with thoughts of how to make her care about him. She was always on his mind. In the best of circumstances, he couldn't think of any reasons a woman like her would want to be with a person like him. And they didn't have the best of circumstances.

On his way over to her office, he knew he was entering foreign territory, so he went to a familiar place. He decided to get her something to eat. She was always forgetting the time and how long it had been since her last meal. That he could do. That he knew how to fix. Everything else was a mystery when it came to her.

She seemed happy enough to see him, and she really enjoyed the *kouign amann*, but he was convinced she didn't need him or his bad intentions in her life. God, she was everything he wanted and couldn't have. Sure, she'd abide by the contract, but she'd never willingly come to him.

She was wearing her hair down and looked beautiful and thoughtful. She was perfect, and he wondered if she would kiss him.

He was always surprised when she said yes.

It was the feeling of her lips on his that set everything right. When she was in his arms and kissing him he thought he could believe in himself. Be a better man.

The long wait, the anticipation, and sleepless nights thinking of her made him approach her. She was all softness in his arms as he snuck a hand behind her waist and another one through the curls of her black hair. He brought her closer and touched his mouth to hers, and like a dream, she responded. He deepened the kiss, demanding everything she had as he slipped his tongue into her mouth. She tasted so sweet, like *kouign amann*, like sugar. Like his Hana.

He pulled away for a moment to say something, because with her, he always wanted more. "I would like to see you when you get back." He gazed into her big brown eyes.

She nodded, and he took her mouth again, knowing he'd be empty the whole time she was gone.

Chapter Seventeen

Hana said goodbye to her apartment and her cat, who was staying with a neighbor. As soon as they were cleared for takeoff, and the wheels of the 757 left the ground, she watched as the city she loved was also left behind. She settled into her seat and clicked off her seatbelt when the seatbelt sign when off. Taron covered herself with a travel blanket and attempted to sleep. With her ears popping, Hana also closed her eyes, but sleep was not going to happen. All she could think about was Adrian. Adrian in her office kissing her and rendering her nonsensical. Adrian letting her know he wanted to see her when she returned

Adrian left alone to his own devices for ninety-two days.

She was skeptical, but had hope. Based on what, she couldn't say. Especially since they were in some sort of weird romantic limbo. That damn contract made everything impossible to gauge. She had to remember they hadn't torn up the contract, but after Lisa walked in on them, something definitely shifted.

She hoped the next three months would help her find clarity and sanity.

Hana found herself in a troubled sleep as she shifted back and forth trying to get comfortable. After the stop at LAX, they still had five more hours of travel time in the air. While Taron caught up on her sleep, Hana couldn't stop herself from overthinking.

Worry over her attachment to a man she shouldn't trust, and hope that her sensibilities hadn't gotten so scrambled she'd lost her sense of self.

Hana had to remind herself again they'd made no commitments. He would and could have any woman in the world. She didn't know if he'd miss her when she wasn't at his beck and call, and she was angry with herself that she cared.

Yet, when she was kissing him, Hana felt like they were connected.

She was being foolish, and was romanticizing a devil's bargain. By the time she came back to San Francisco, he'd be a mistake she made, but a boon to Esperanza. She'd be nothing more than a memory for him, and a small dent in his financial portfolio.

She opened her eyes, from this point on she'd have to put him out of her mind. She'd have to completely forget about Adrian and live her life for herself. She couldn't spend the next three months worrying about him and whether he cared for her. It was time to admit that she deserved better than Adrian Douglas.

When the wheels of the Airbus touched down in La Aurora, Hana and Taron went to baggage claim where they met up with a few of the construction people working with Esperanza. They all piled into a SUV, and rode for six hours until they reached their destination. Hana was grateful for the fatigue. She had enough energy to clean up and then pass out in her narrow bed. When her head hit the pillow, she was dead to the world.

The next morning, her feet hit the ground as soon as she opened her eyes. She and Taron got to work and didn't get back until midnight. Then, she was pushed food down her throat, cleaned up and went to sleep. Rinse, repeat, and repeat again. She didn't turn on her phone on until day three.

Five messages popped up and went from a friendly tone of asking if she'd arrived safe to was she okay, and then turned overly polite when Adrian asked if she would please communicate when she was able.

For him, that was reasonable behavior. She kept expecting him to show up for some reason. Stupid magical thinking, she believe she could conjure him with her mind. She kind of wished he was here, if for no other reason than to see him getting his suits dirty while travelling in the back of trucks. She sent him a message acknowledging she'd arrived safe, then she shut off her phone.

Unbidden, every time a particularly tall gentleman walked around the corner, she waited until she saw his face to confirm it wasn't Adrian. She shook off the odd feeling of him not being there. The Esperanza team were too busy collecting supplies and going over blue prints for her to dwell on it, but a couple thoughts about him slipped in every day.

The work was hard, the humidity was oppressive, and by the end of every day, she was bone tired. They seemed to carry, and transport supplies more than they did anything else, and she went to bed every night feeling like a lifeless shell of a human being. But, as was always the case, all their efforts had great rewards. After two weeks, they'd built one entire school and broke ground on the others. There was nothing like walking around and seeing the transformation with her own eyes.

At least she didn't spend the nights like a lovesick insomniac. Occasionally, she would get texts from Adrian and she'd send him a quick text back sharing information about the builds. Nothing personal. Never personal.

He, on the other hand, "talked" to her in the texts, which was unsettling. It wasn't like him, and it gave her hope she knew she was an idiot to have.

***

Adrian was not happy, Hana's texts were perfunctory, and were sent only in response to his. He missed her. He wanted her here. Certainly no farther than the other side of the city where he could pop in—she hated when he did that— to tempt her to go to dinner with him. He went to work and pretended he was happy for her and the children the schools would help. Actually, he was pleased, but he saw no reason she had to be there to make all that happen.

He wanted to throw more money at her and tell her to hire more people so she could come back early. The schools would still be built. She could even see daily progress with photos and video. But, he knew, it was important for her to be there.

In her absence, he was learning a lot about her, and about himself. Of all things, he found himself wondering about Pumpkin, who must be lonely for her too.

He didn't know who was taking care of her cat. If she had asked, he would've sent Louis to go check on the poor creature. He texted her and she didn't respond for two days. That was the way of it with her these days.

He wanted to fly over and visit her, but decided his impatience and forceful nature would make her like him even less than she did now. That was a line he found he didn't want to cross, even if he worried every day that she might be meeting the love of her life. A stranger, who would appear when she needed him, helping her build the schools, holding her as she climbed a ladder, and getting ever so close to her. It would be probably be some altruistic druid who recently returned from backpacking around Asia. He would be sickeningly well-cultured and probably steal naïve Hana's heart.

Somebody had to tell her to watch out for guys like that, but Adrian knew somebody should have told her about guys like him.

He returned to the thought of Hana's poor cat. The overweight orange thing that lived in her apartment. Leaving it behind was really was appalling. The poor creature was probably waiting every day like a fool for her return while she met her next boyfriend. Adrian hadn't thought to put in an exclusivity clause in the contract, and now he was kicking himself that he didn't. He texted her to see if he could check up on the cat every day, asking if she would be all right with him entering her apartment. He was trying to learn about boundaries.

Chapter Eighteen

Hana looked down at her phone and broke out laughing. Taron was talking to her, and Hana looked up, but she was still shaking her head and smiling.

"So, I see you are still with your billionaire boyfriend," Taron said, and continued walking down the street of the small town. They'd purchased groceries, but found themselves window shopping. Hana had stopped to re-read her text and when she looked up she saw Taron staring at her.

Hana had stolen a few moments to text Adrian and felt guilty about it. She'd told herself she was leaving him behind, and here she was, behaving like a high school girl texting the most popular boy in the class.

But she liked Adrian like this. One text at a time, he reminded her there was more to their connection than sex. And the distance gave her an opportunity to process her emotions without him hovering, or standing in her doorway, or tempting her.

Even though they hadn't seen or spoken to each other, she felt like she was connected to him.

"He wants to check on my cat," Hana stated, looking into Taron's eyes. "If you knew him, you'd understand how funny that was."

He hated her cat. That Adrian wanted to check on Pumpkin might be an indication he was changing his ways. She may be an incurable romantic, but it felt like Adrian was acting differently.

Answering Taron's earlier question, Hana said, "I guess I'm still seeing him. Though, a lot can happen in three months."

She tried to sound like it didn't matter what happened when she got back, that she could take him or leave him. She hadn't told Taron the circumstances of Adrian's donation, and Hana didn't think she ever would. The secret hung guiltily over Hana's head every moment she spent with her best friend.

"He really saved Esperanza," Taron said soberly.

Hana could tell Taron hated the reason she believed Adrian had donated the money. What Bianca did still burned, and Hana understood that feeling. In some ways, she was still numb, and she hadn't really grieved the loss. She'd been too distracted by everything Adrian to process the enormity of what Bianca did and to pay attention how Taron was doing.

Even now, Taron sounded angry and morose, and Hana felt like a terrible friend.

Taron had stopped in front of a stall and was absentmindedly picking up little ceramic items and looking at them.

Hana could never tell Taron why he had given them the money. She was too ashamed of herself for taking it, and repulsed that Adrian had offered. Even if there were some slim bouts of affection between them now, how that came to be made it impossible for her to share with her best friend.

Most of all, Hana worried that Taron knew the truth somehow and was going to talk to her about it. She still didn't have the courage to face the conversation she knew they needed to have.

"He did," Hana agreed. His money did save their charity. But in no way were they indebted to him. Truly, he got his pound of flesh out of the bargain. Every night and every day, she wished they could've support Esperanza another way.

"And I hate that," Taron said, looking at Hana and echoing her thoughts, though for entirely different reasons.

Taron understood her better than any other person in the world how it felt to have to rely on donors to keep Esperanza running. Always, absolutely, always, they had their hands out begging. Now, after what Bianca did to them, without Adrian's money, Esperanza would've died.

Like Hana, Taron was happiest when they completed building another school. They wanted to run the charity on their own terms, but that wasn't how non-profits worked.

"I hate it too," Hana admitted. "I hate Bianca for what she did to us."

"I do too," Taron declared, her tone harsh. "If I ever catch that perra…" She let her threat trail off.

Hana nodded. "I'd help you too." Hana hugged her best friend and said, "I love you, T."

"I love you, too," Taron replied. She smiled and walked away and Hana followed.

The evening was mild, and there was a light breeze. Warm summery air was blowing against her hair, and she allowed it to soothe her. It would be a long time before Taron shook off the shroud Bianca laid over Esperanza, and Hana was committed to helping her friend get through the worst of it.

"I hate being dependent on a man," Taron said suddenly, breaking the silence. "Or on anyone really. After what happened with Bianca, I've been struggling with how we can keep Esperanza going."

"What can we do but take in donations?" Hana asked. "We're a non-profit organization. Donors are our bread and butter."

Bianca had shaken their trust and faith in Esperanza, and Taron was struggling.

"I want us to diversify," Taron said with determination. She followed behind Hana as she walked into the fabric section of the market. This was Hana's happy place. Everyday Taron let Hana spend time picking through the goods while fantasizing what yarns she wanted to buy. Hana always ended up taking home or mailing home yards of fabric from wherever she went in. She got lost in the search of colorful cuts of fiber as Taron stood nearby.

"In what way," Hana began, "would you like to see us change? In the way we fundraise or the way we operate?"

"The way we get our money," Taron said firmly. "I want us to be more proactive but in a way that is personal to us." Hana wanted that too. Taron held up the textile Hana had been holding. She had been two seconds away from buying that particular piece of fabric. "Sell our own goods that we design."

"Like from my sewing?" Hana asked skeptically. "You know I make robes for myself, and I'm not very good. I really love the patterns on that." Hana pointed to the fabric Taron was holding. "No one would buy anything we made."

The textile was interesting. Hana studied the pattern of alternating stripes of pink and teal with a heart of bright orange in the middle of the design. The colors and shapes in the woven fabric spoke to her. Hana had the strong urge to sew something with it, create something out of it.

"What I love is that they've been doing this for centuries," Taron said, turning over the fabric and inspecting it. "You can see the Mayan influence in this. This is special. Besides how many robes have you made for me? People love your robes."

Hana agreed the fabric was special. "I've seen them make it. The women use coal and clay and leaves to create these colors. How do you see this fitting into Esperanza?"

"It's beautiful is all I'm saying." Taron continued, "I've been thinking a lot of people back home might like to buy this too."

Hana smiled at her. "You want to go into business selling clothes?" She shook her head. "What about our schools? I don't want us to get distracted from what's really important."

Taron had an answer for that. "Every dime we make from the clothes will go into Esperanza." She was talking about supporting the charity with the sales from a for-profit company. It would change the entire nature of what they did.

"We already have a business," Hana reminded her. They didn't have time to start a second one.

Taron turned around. "Hana, I want to start a genuine business so that we can fund our charity. It's time for a change. No more Bianca and no more Adrian. We have to do this for ourselves." Taron had a point. Hana knew what Taron was asking, that they start over after everything had gone to hell. Start the hard journey of creating a business that poured its profits into Esperanza.

"Hana," Taron called, meeting Hana's gaze, then taking her hands. "Will you start a business with me?"

Hana looked at her best friend. "You want to sell clothes with me?" she asked.

"Or purses or pillows, or anything else you want. I want to raise money with you, Hana," Taron stated. "For our charity, by ourselves."

Hana shook her head. "I don't want to exploit these people," Hana said. "I want to do this right. We can't expect someone to make our product and not make real money doing it. I want them to be partners. Everyone needs to make a profit."

"They'll be the stars of our product." Taron said and nodded. "People will buy it because of them. We help support the communities where we build our schools and put the profits of the sales of the product in Esperanza."

"Exactly. We spread the love."

Chapter Nineteen

It turned out to be ninety-five days when Hana got on a plane and headed back to California. She texted Adrian during her layover in LAX that she was physically back in the United States. He responded immediately asking for her flight number.

She texted it to him and turned off her phone. Hana felt more exhausted getting back to San Francisco than she did leaving it. Getting home was always difficult. It took some time to adjust to whatever country they'd been in, and once they got busy, Hana got absorbed by the culture, the people, and the pace of that life. Arriving back in the U.S. was a jolt to the system, and recalibrating her rhythm always took some time.

Now, she faced a whole other layer upon her return home. Anticipation, nerves, and expectation all around seeing Adrian again. As if it would make a difference, after they landed at SFO, she waited a moment to turn on her phone.

Hana looked over at Taron with grateful eyes. After three months, she was ready for a taxi ride to her apartment, her cat, and most importantly her bed. She didn't know where Adrian and she stood, but Hana knew where she wanted to be standing. Under hot water in her shower. She was tired, jetlagged, and disoriented.

Hana hugged Taron at the baggage claim as she left to go home.

Hana walked out of the airport and into the sunlight, hoping to do the same. She rolled her luggage down the walkway as people passed, and stopped dead in her tracks when she saw a familiar face in the crowd. Louis, the driver, in his charcoal gray suit and tie.

She shielded her eyes from the sun bouncing off the hood of Adrian's black car, as Louis rested against it. Adrian rolled down the window and poked his head out to look at her.

"Ms. Romero," he called in a slow drawl.

It felt like the sunlight lit her heart. She hadn't known how much she missed that stupid arrogant face until she saw it looking at her.

Her Adrian. His bright emerald eyes sparkled as he hung his head out the window and grinned at her. Louis took her bag and headed for the trunk as Adrian opened the door for her to get in. She shook her head but didn't argue. She had missed him.

"Mr. Douglas," she returned.

Hana got into the car and closed the door. She looked down as she settled into the seat and buckled her seatbelt. She was nervous being this close to Adrian again. She waited then looked up at him. Hunger shone bright and clear in his eyes, the vert color twinkling and his lips twitched with a contained smile. His blond hair, combed to the side, was so light and angelic.

As always, he was dressed impeccably. He wore a dark carbon suit, tailored to his waist and clinging to his muscled arms. Hana knew he had dressed up for her. She let her eyes rest on his full lips, and the anticipation of having those lips on hers made her squirm.

She felt the car shift from park to drive, and without thought she found herself attacking Adrian. Like no time had passed, she couldn't get enough of him. Right then and there, she decided, he was hers, with or without a contract.

Hana grabbed the back of his head and pulled him to her. There were no words, only her lips on his. It was easy enough to forget the last three months had ever happened, and the dark bargain that had introduced them.

Hana lost herself in the feeling of his mouth on hers as he matched each press of her lips with a demand of his own. Their tongues dueled, and she shivered with anticipation of what was to come. All of her moral objections were reduced to ash as his kiss burned her mouth.

***

When Hana kissed him, Adrian's heart stopped in his chest. He couldn't breathe, he couldn't think, he could only feel. The soft pillowy touch of her mouth as it pressed against his lips was the most delicious thing he'd ever felt. Sweet, beautiful Hana was in his arms again with her hands in his hair. She was back from saving the world to finally save him properly.

She was kissing him as desperately as he was kissing her, and he claimed her with his mouth again and again. He promised himself only a kiss, but got drunk on the feeling of knowing it wasn't enough. When he saw her walking through the airport exit doors, he knew with absolute certainty he was head over heels in love.

Her kiss confirmed it.

He was forever changed by this woman's kiss. He hadn't asked her to dance that night, she had called to him like a siren. He hadn't invited her to his house, she had come to claim him. He knew all of this and didn't care as long as he could have her always.

Adrian would stake his fortune on making her his.

He kissed her again in a way that communicated he would never let her go. He pulled back to look at her. She had stars in her beautiful brown eyes, and he knew it was arrogant, but he knew only he could make her feel this way.

"I need a shower," she said, putting her hand on his chest.

She looked like she had been thoroughly kissed, her full lips swollen and red. Her dark hair was falling down her shoulders in a wave of uncontrolled curls. He delighted in the effect he had on her.

Adrian nodded. "You can take a shower," he said, but he had a sin-filled strategy to get her in his arms again.

He brushed the curls back from her face, he would absolutely let Hana take a shower. He planned to get her straight home to his apartment, where he would help her get cleaned up.

Adrian didn't know how to win her heart yet, but at least he knew how to give her pleasure. Until he figured out what he needed to do to show her he could and would be what she needed him to be, he intended to torture them in any way possible.

***

Hana had her hands against the glass shower wall. The water rained over her head and hair, and steam rose over the tops of their heads. Adrian was behind her reminding her he'd missed ninety plus days of being without her. His devilish fingers worked their magic as he claimed her. He caressed her shoulder with a whisper light touch as he pulled the hair back from her neck, then put his sinful mouth on the crook of her nape and suckled at the wet flesh. Though he was kissing her in one spot, she could feel the pleasure everywhere as her head fell back onto his chest. It felt so right being in the cage of his strong biceps.

Only Adrian, could make getting clean feel so naughty.

The water jetted down her face as pleasure stole her breath. He was caressing her up and down the length of her arms and building sweet anticipation. She tilted up her face for a kiss, and he complied as his hand made its way to her breast. She moaned into his mouth. She missed these hands. Adrian cupped one aching breast and gave it his adoring attention, pulling and massaging until she felt the fever rising.

The water ran over his hands as he pinched her aching nipple. The flesh smarted under his wicked fingers. She wanted him badly. She could feel the desire pooling at the base of her hips and his hard cock pressing against her bottom. Feeling his desire turned her on even more. She lifted her hands up on the glass again and surrendered. She never felt more ready for him. Adrian found her throbbing entrance, and he pressed home with one urgent thrust.

Impaled on pleasure, Hana screamed. Adrian made love to her with such passion and determination, it made her senseless. He pumped in and out of her and she swore he felt bigger than she remembered, his girth stretching her gloriously. He was using his whole body to finish what his pleasure-filled kisses had started.

The fire burned hotter as she began to chase her release. The water cascaded down their bodies as she met him thrust for thrust and demanded her climax.

***

Adrian feasted on Hana's kiss. Before she left, he'd though he could never get enough of her, but now he *knew* that was a fact, not a feeling. Every time he made love to her, he felt like it was better than the last time, more perfect. He was always left with the taste of wanting more of her. He could still savor the taste of her kiss long after she stopped making love to his mouth.

He put his hand on hers as she clutched the shower wall, thrusting his cock in and out of her sex, driving deeper with every jolt of his hips, demanding she finish before him, and used his fingers to ensure it. His legs were entwined with hers as he massaged her clit.

Hana held his forearm like she was holding on for dear life. He rubbed the engorged bud with an unrelenting circular motion, the action lubricated by the shower.

He felt her convulsing around his cock, and her hips thrust back, bucking with her climax. He tried to last, to savor her a little longer, but with her perfect soft body in his hands and her wet and tight sheath around him, he couldn't endure the desire any longer. One last deep thrust sent him over the edge. He found his release and buried his face in the crook of her neck as he fought to catch his breath.

Only Hana could do this to him. She sent him to heaven every time he had her in his arms. He turned off the shower and held her close until the air started to cool. Then he took her out of the shower, dried her from her top to toe, then lifted her in his arms and brought her into his bedroom where he made love to her again on his bed. And then on the floor beside his bed. He wouldn't rest until she screamed out his name.

They finished on the floor, their chests heaving. Hana turned her head to face him and looked into his eyes. He felt like she was looking into his soul.

"Without that contract," she whispered, "without be *paid* to be with you, we could've had something real."

The sting of her words seeped deep into Adrian's bones. He couldn't believe she didn't think there was anything real between them. He couldn't disagree more. He had a sea of emotions rolling around in his body. He'd never experienced the levels of passion he reached with her. Every tortuous minute of being apart had made life intolerable. He'd consoled himself by getting her cat from her neighbor, taking it to her apartment and feeding the fat orange tabby he commiserated with on a daily basis. Pumpkin was as lovesick as Adrian was.

He'd spent the last ninety days of his life lost in the memories of her smile and the sound of her laughter. She'd charmed him body and soul, and he craved her. When she got into the car and he was able to touch her, he nearly swooned like a stupid schoolgirl.

From the moment she'd flown thousands of miles away from him, he was besieged by thoughts of truly having Hana as his girlfriend, and then, maybe more. He didn't know what more entailed, but if it contained more making love with her, laughing with her, and the sweet healing cure of her kiss, he would jump headfirst into the vast unknown.

All he felt was real and had nothing to do with money or a contract. He hated that he'd made the offer. He hated that she couldn't see past it, and his heart started bleeding at the loss of his deluded dreams of a future of resplendent bliss when she shared her resentment.

His reverie was slipping from his fingers, his time with Hana was running out. He would be inconsolably desolate when she left him for good, but he couldn't blame her. After what he did, he deserved to be alone.

Yes, he was a bad man. He'd done vile things to get Hana in his bed. But he wasn't sorry he'd gotten to indulge in the fantasy of what being with her could be like. He would never regret what he'd done since it brought him here. In love with her.

The hell of it was he could never make her love him. He would never be able to make her forget his mistakes. His lungs ached. He couldn't catch his breath. He looked at the ceiling experiencing something new and horrible. He felt vulnerable.

He turned his head to meet her gaze. "You wouldn't have said yes to me any other way," he told her.

Hana didn't need him, his money, or his greedy, selfish soul in her life. Guilt made his heart hurt so badly, now he knew what angina felt like.

He hated himself.

Her chest heaved and her voice shook when she said, "But now that we've done this, I can never look at you the same way, and Adrian, I wanted to. I really did."

He looked over at the largest saucers of sad brown eyes he had ever seen. He'd wanted to believe he picked up his girlfriend, the love of his life, from the airport, brought her home, and showed her how much he missed her. Instead he'd given her ten million reasons to hate him.

"I wanted to be with you," he said quietly. He put a hand out to touch her face. "I still do." He wanted to say *long after you'd tired of me. Long after this year. Long after you left me forever.*

Hana turned her face away from his hand and broke his heart when she said, "I'm going to go home now."

He nodded, watched her get up, and leave the room. A few minutes later, he heard her luggage on the tiles, and then the front door closing.

He was lying naked on the floor long after she left.

Empty and bereft.

Chapter Twenty

Adrian had a problem. Usually, he was skilled at solving problems, but with each passing day he found the solution to this particular situation hopeless. His clothes from the night she came home were still strewn on the floor. He paced around his home in his favorite dark blue silk robe.

His sheets felt cold as he climbed onto the bed and pulled his laptop onto the comforter. He tried to work, but couldn't. He wasn't functioning normally.

Adrian looked down at his phone. Hana had sent him a text. She asked if he could give her the name of a good attorney. After not hearing from her or talking to her for days, this is what she wanted from him? The only reason she'd want a lawyer was to find out if she was able to break the contract.

He shouldn't be surprised. The money would always be between them, and more horrendously, he'd taken advantage of her at her weakest moment. That would be the toxic miasma that always hung over them.

But he wanted what he had *never* wanted before. He wanted Hana to commit to him, only to him, and love him for the rest of their lives.

So, he had an idea.

***

Hana unlocked the door to her apartment and dropped a ton of bags at the door. Pumpkin greeted her, something he'd rarely done before she left on this trip. She had so many product samples she and Taron were experimenting with, and was overwhelmed with how many options there were. Between an endless supply of different patterns and hundreds of possible designs, all from developing countries, somewhere Esperanza had built schools, Hana decided they needed to focus on one product. They'd contacted several agencies and chose one that contracted seamstresses in the regions from which the fabrics were sourced to fashion the prototypes. Taron and Hana were pleased with the initial results, but had to focus on one product to kick off the line.

She collapsed onto the couch and started thinking about Adrian, and how she'd asked him for a lawyer, and how he'd sent a list of ten. She and Taron were doing something they never had done before: going into business to make money. She didn't have enough experience in for-profit companies, so the attorney she chose would help them with incorporating, their business plan, and what they'd need to do to fund the company.

Taron and Hana needed to actualize this pipe dream properly if she was ever going to consider a future with Adrian, which was so up in the air, she needed time and space to figure out if they could make it work, and how that would happen given their inauspicious beginning.

Hana needed to concentrate on one thing at a time. Taron had too many brilliant ideas and Hana would have to reign in her friend's creativity. Hana cautioned that the fledgling project shouldn't handle the production of too many items, but Taron had twenty different ideas for purses, dresses, suits, and hats. Hana worried Taron's vision was too big.

Hana hadn't told Adrian about the business. She didn't say why she needed an attorney. She intended to keep all the details to herself until they launched the company. Then she'd set up a payment schedule to return the one million dollars she'd committed to Esperanza. The rest was still sitting in the bank, waiting to return to its owner.

Mind moves matter. She found herself thinking about their new business concept everyday while sitting at her desk at Esperanza. Taron agonized over the details in Hana's office by day, and they kept each other up on the phone half the night.

Looking at Pumpkin, she got up and poured some kibbles into a bowl, but didn't make anything for herself. She didn't have time to eat. She picked up her phone and called Taron. She had another question.

"How are we going to source the fabric in bulk if they make it in small batches?"

"You should be worrying how we're going to package the pieces after they get here," Taron stated. She could hear the sounds of laughter and music. Hana had obviously interrupted Taron's night, and remembered she'd mentioned a date.

"I'm working on logistics. I spent all day scouting factories in zip codes we can't afford," Hana said, collapsing on the couch. She had a plan to rent one, but coming up with the money for the deposit, the rent, and the machinery was a behemoth of an obstacle. She'd begun a slew of interviews that had people rotating in and out her office. She had found a couple of promising candidates to work in their non-existent warehouse, and knew she was jumping the gun, but couldn't seem to contain her enthusiasm. Well, until she spoke to the lawyer who brought her down to earth, where she crash-landed once being reminded of the financial realities.

She asked her friend, "Did we bite off more than we can chew?"

Taron didn't answer immediately, and the silence confirmed all Hana's worries.

"Mind moves matter," Taron reminded her.

Yeah, but they'd have to be successful if she was going to pay back Adrian. One day soon she wanted to write him a check as the first installment in a payment plan. She didn't need his money, and if they could survive overcoming their messed-up start then maybe there was hope for a real relationship.

Hana nodded. "I trust you, T."

"You know, we talked about this in Guatemala, and women we met on the trip are giving me projections and referrals. There're a lot of women who might want to become contractors," she continued, sort of yelling over the background noise. "Each bag, and I say we focus on bags, could have a label with the names of the women who created it."

Hana agreed. "Let's go with that," she said sleepily looking at all the tester handbags she had set by the door. She loved all the samples that had been mocked up, including the different shapes of the bags they'd created in a selection of fabrics they had fallen in love with. She liked the simple shoulder bag and the slouchy hobo the best.

Taron and Hana had met quite a few women in Guatemala who had been eager at the prospect of extra income—real income—and their wares were undeniably special. Taron had seen this in other locally sourced lines, and wanted to adopt it in theirs: each artisan would be showcased in every purchase. Each tag would have the woman's name who made the fabric and the name of the woman who assembled the parts of the handbag. The tag would highlight the real people behind each product, and each hand that touched it. Hana was excited to hire predominantly women. It was a cause special and dear to her heart to financially enable women, especially in emerging countries.

That's why Adrian's bargain was anathema to everything Hana knew about herself. Every day since she'd signed she hated herself for having done it.

The flip side of that was, she'd come to have genuine feelings for Adrian. She couldn't deny what did to her in the bedroom, but she'd never give him her heart if she didn't pay him back. She kept Adrian at bay figuring if he could stand to wait for her, he could have her. Hana knew she was worth waiting for, but Adrian wasn't a man accustomed to delayed gratification.

After she hung up the phone she let much needed sleep claim her even though she was contorted on her sofa. Her neck would pay, but Hana was too tired to care.

She fell asleep thinking of her light haired, green-eyed debauched Romeo, her degenerate Mr. Darcy.

Her indecent Prince Charming.

Chapter Twenty-One

In the morning light, Hana blinked her eyes open and stared at the slitted pupils of a particularly plump orange tabby. Hana chuckled at him, then groaned. Her neck resisted attempts to straighten out. She rubbed the sore spot as she swung her legs to sit up. She took a couple of over-the-counter pain meds, and then hopped in the shower, thinking of Adrian. Again.

Hana rubbed a washcloth all over her body, mimicking the motions he'd made. It was easy to remember Adrian's hands all over her, touching the same sensitive places she was washing now. She ran the cloth over her breasts, tingling with awareness and need. He certainly had a way with his hands, and she liked the feel of him.

Hana loved rubbing her hands down his chest and lower as the drops fell from her fingers. She had a hankering for him, a strong one. No matter how revolting their agreement was, she couldn't deny how it felt to be with him. Their sex was combustive, and that first night she was back they'd made love, and it was a revelation.

Hana wanted him, no matter how depraved and corrupt he was, but she'd continue to show restraint. She couldn't have him right now, and she didn't know if she could have him at all. He was damn expensive, both financially and emotionally.

She finished her shower nowhere near as satisfied as she wanted to be. She'd need a strong coffee in a cup large enough to hold at least twenty-four ounces.

When she finally walked into her office she slumped into her chair. She was still wearing her sunglasses when Taron walked in a moment later. She looked much worse. She was wearing a black jumpsuit and her hair was spiky and slept on. Except Taron didn't look like she had slept. The circles under her eyes were large and she was yawning as she sat down in front of Hana's desk. There was a carafe for four coffees, and Hana had already finished one and had abandoned it on the desk with the cap off. She had her second cup held firmly in her hand.

She waved to the remaining two, took off her sunglasses and revealed her own eye bags. “Please be my guest.”

Taron smiled and took one, sucking back deep gulps like it was water. “So, what’s the plan for the day, boss?”

Hana sat up. “We’re going to see a warehouse. How was your date?”

Taron pursed her lips and described her night. “She wasn’t thrilled I was sweet-talking with you.” Taron said, sardonically. “She said it sounded like we were flirting.”

“That’s unfortunate.” Though sorta true. They’d been best friends for so long their verbal short-hand probably sounded cute or ridiculous. Hana shrugged apologetically. “Sorry, T.”

“I didn’t say she didn’t come home with me.” Taron laughed and raised her coffee to toast her. “To burning the midnight oil.”

Hana chuckled then told Taron the plans for the day. “We’re going to see a warehouse.”

When they arrived at the imposing brick building, Hana knew in her heart that this would be a great starter home for them. They’d be able to grow into this space. Even if they surpassed the best growth models, it’d be years before they’d need to expand. Since Hana never shared “the contract” with Taron, explaining where she got the money to move ahead with the warehouse would be problematic. As was dipping into more of Adrian’s money. The mental war Hana waged had her resigned to paying him back for a longer period of time, unless their business they decided to call T+H, took off in a big way.

Hana led Taron into the warehouse. As she opened the door, Hana took in the soaring ceilings and the vast open space. In that space she saw possibility. The bright light of day shone through long windows high up on the walls, and bounced off the steel supports, illuminating the room.

Hana couldn’t wait to start making the bags they’d agreed on. She’d learned that type of merchandise was the most pre-ordered product on retail websites. Their lawyer had not only helped them form their business and business model, but also counseled them to skip the expensive store front and instead focus on online sales.

Online sales would be more profitable, and for the first time, Hana was all about the money: earning it, saving it, and purchasing only enough property for them to work in. This place would be perfect for them.

"We can't afford this," Taron said in a worshipful whisper. Hana knew that meant she loved it. Taron was almost never speechless.

"Yes, we can," Hana said firmly. "We already did." The offer had been accepted and the money was cleared. Taron better love it.

"Is this really ours?" Taron marveled, looking over the vast space. It was similar to the feeling they'd had when they'd rented their first place for Esperanza. Moving out of Taron's family garage had been the highlight of their lives. Now life was becoming more expansive with their first warehouse.

Hana nodded. She pointed to the right, a place where she imagined rows of sewing machines that would be people driven. "We're going to put the bags together here." She led Taron by the hand to the open area in the back. "This can be where we package everything and get it ready for shipping."

Taron laughed and spun around. "Should we paint in pink or blue?"

Hana shook her head and put her hand on her hips. She said. "As long as our baby is profitable, I don't care."

"I thought you didn't care about money," Taron said, raising a brow.

"I didn't, I don't," Hana explained. "But I see all this as being about raising our own money for Esperanza."

Taron regarded her as if she were searching for the reason Hana has swung "to the dark side." "Do you feel like you have to be with Adrian because of the money?"

It was more like she *couldn't* be with Adrian because of the money.

"I want to pay him back," she admitted. It had never sat right with Taron either. She didn't know how Hana had gotten the money, but Taron knew she didn't want a man supporting their charity when they could do it on their own. Taron knew that Hana didn't like being indebted to Adrian, which was how she felt: indebted. She didn't want to be the kind of woman who was with a man because he'd paid her bills. She wanted to recapture the woman who had the *cajones* to start a charity and make it thrive. If it hadn't been for

Bianca, Hana would've never stooped as low as she did when she accepted Adrian's offer.

"You will, Hana. We will," Taron promised.

Chapter Twenty-Two

Hana let herself into her apartment carrying one of Taron's newest prototypes on her back: a colorful backpack, which she carefully set down on her coffee table next the bagels she'd run out to get this morning. She sat on her couch and looked at the backpack for a couple of moments, full of wonder. She could remember their conversation in Guatemala clearly, holding up the same pink, teal, and orange accent fabric and wondering if they could do it. Now they were designing backpacks with the same fabric.

She was proud of what they had been able to accomplish so far, and saw the possibilities expanding before her. She wouldn't need Adrian to or any other donor to help them build schools. T+H would be the vehicle they'd use to do it themselves.

A knock on her door cut through her thoughts, and she grinned somehow knowing it was Adrian. Hana really could conjure him if she thought about him long enough.

It'd been two weeks since she'd returned from Guatemala. Two weeks since they'd had an amazing reunion, then she walked out of his penthouse and hadn't been back.

When she opened the door and saw him standing there, she wasn't surprised. He looked like trouble incarnate. Her gaze travelled over his full lips and his finely muscled body showcased under the expert tailoring of his black suit. She admired his biceps and thick thighs. No getting around the fact he was an impressive male specimen. Holding something exceedingly feminine. A large arrangement of white-pink peonies.

Flowers? She thought Adrian didn't do romance. He walked in and she closed the door so Pumpkin wouldn't escape.

"Sorry I didn't call," he said, with the grace to actually look contrite. "I came to give you these."

He stood near the door, not moving into the room. It wasn't unusual for them to jump each other as soon as the door closed. His demeanor screamed restraint and she wondered why that was about at the same time she appreciated the change-up.

"Thank you." She couldn't help but smile while looking at the peonies. "Only to drop them off?" she took the flowers from his hand as he rocked back on his heels.

"Louis is waiting for me," he said.

Huh. After two weeks of no more than a couple of texts about lawyers, no insisting she explain herself or her whereabouts. No pushing her against the wall and taking what he wanted, even if she was always a willing participant.

Okay, this was freaking her out in an entirely different way. A chivalrous, sweet gift from a man whose idea of a fairytale was giving her money for sex. She was touched, and felt a little shy.

She motioned to her bright orange couch. "Would you like to sit with me for a few minutes?"

"I'd love that," he said, nodding. He brushed a gentle kiss to her forehead then walked over to her living room area. It was a welcome caress that made her long to be in his arms. Confusing watching him engage in self-restraint. She was more than a little curious to see how this played out.

"Would you like a cup of tea?" She asked from the kitchen as she snipped the ends off the flowers and put them in a vase of water.

"That would be lovely," he answered and sat on her couch. Pumpkin perched next to him, and she waited for Adrian to shoo the cat away. Instead, Pumpkin was giving Adrian head rubs in his hand, and Adrian murmuring to her cat.

Okay. This was veering into weird.

She started the kettle and considered the man who looked, sounded, and dressed like Adrian, but was sitting contentedly on the couch communing with Pumpkin. She watched them as she waited for the pot to whistle. When it did, she made up two Earl Greys, then joined Adrian on the couch.

"How was your day?" he asked, sipping the tea out of one of her porcelain cups, which seemed perfectly suited in his aristocratic hands.

Who was this guy? She eyed him suspiciously. He didn't try anything, and seemed...respectful.

"Busy, and then became sort of...eventful." She chuckled. "How was yours?"

He put his teacup back in its matching saucer. “Much better now that I’ve seen you.”

She smiled. He really was putting on the charm. Conversation failed her as she sipped at her tea, it had been a long day and she was getting tired. Tired of hating Adrian, resenting Adrian, fighting not to love Adrian. Not to mention, she was physically fatigued and didn’t have the wits to be careful around him. He was tempting all the time, but this visit? Making nice and acting like an old-fashioned gentleman suitor—a sweet fantasy to indulge in.

“Can I hold your hand?” he asked quietly and looked down. She hadn’t expected that. It was the tamest thing they’d ever done. She knew the contours of his body better than the shape of his hands. She’d slept with him before ever having a dinner date. Holding his hand now would be like having had the dessert then the appetizer.

***

Adrian looked up at Hana when she didn’t answer right away. He couldn’t take being away from her another minute and gambled on her being home, letting him in, accepting his flowers, talking to him... All of it. As precarious as he felt this moment was, he was hang gliding, and coasting on the thermals by merely being in her presence.

With a cocked eyebrow, she considered him. She put down her teacup and placed it on the coffee table. As she leaned down to set it on the table, Adrian glanced at the revealed cleavage as the fabric of her shirt pulled across her chest. He refocused on her heart-shaped face. Her dark curly hair fell into her eyes, and his fingers itched to brush it back behind her ear. Her sweet lips were pursed as she assessed him silently. He was prepared for rejection. The devastating beauty had every right to tell him to leave, and every time she didn’t it blew his mind.

Hana placed her small hand on his, and Adrian turned his palm up and laced their fingers together. He gave her a small smile. Maybe she hadn’t given up on him yet. Hana smiled back and turned from facing him to sitting next to him. Her small form settled into his side and although he’d had her in so many different ways, these touches were the most intimate he ever felt. When she leaned her head on his shoulder and closed her eyes, he had to hold back the sob in his throat, squeezed up from the compression in his chest at their connection.

Adrian looked down and watched as Hana fell asleep on his shoulder. He relaxed under the soft sounds of her gentle snoring. Pumpkin walked over Adrian's lap, and he let the creature knead at his suit, tearing up the delicate woven fabric of his pants. He rested his head on the top of Hana's and his around her shoulders.

With absolute certainty, he knew he wanted this in his life forever. He wasn't used to these quiet moments, but he could get used to them. The stillness of trust as she slept against him made him feel like he'd conquered the world. He spent the afternoon wondering if what he had planned would work. This was no longer a case of he wanted a taste of her, or he wanted a girlfriend. He needed her in a way he'd never experienced, and he hoped what he had to offer would be enough for her to stay with him for the rest of their lives.

He hated to wake her, but her phone had gone off eight times—Taron had called three times and callers from five local numbers rang in between—and it was near sunset.

Hana opened her sleepy eyes, looked up at him and sighed. "This was nice."

He couldn't disagree. There was no else in the world he would rather be right now. He didn't need to make love to her to be around her. It was soothing to sit with her, pass the time in comfortable silence.

When she leaned her face up to kiss him, the soft touch of her lips made him gasp. He didn't expect the kiss, and he had to hold himself together. It was tempting not to crush her to him and start touching her everywhere. He forced himself to simply treasure the feeling of her mouth on his. Gently, he pressed his lips on hers and sealed them over her mouth. The kiss touched the depths of his soul, and he opened his heart hoping she felt all the need, love, and desire he felt for her.

After drinking deeply of her mouth, she pulled back and regarded him, her gaze searching his face. When she said softly, "You could stay the night," she nearly undid him.

His favorite thing in the world was making love to Hana, but something told him not to. He tried to ignore the stiffening of his pants, and the urge to have her. He closed his eyes and took a breath. "I promised myself I wouldn't," he said with his eyes still closed.

"Why?"

Her question, asked with incredulity threatened to snap his sanity.

He opened his eyes. Beautiful Hana. He didn't deserve her, but he worshipped her. If she told him tomorrow that she never wanted to see him again, he'd spend the rest of his life regretting not trying to keep her. She deserved far more romance than flowers. He swore to ask her to dance with him again, and thought to whirl her around her tiny apartment. It didn't matter where they were, it mattered that she was in his arms. He'd pull out all the romantic stops for her, but for tonight, he had to leave.

If he didn't, he couldn't trust himself not to blow the fragile peace and intimacy they'd found today..

He kissed her softly on the lips once more, tempting fate and his resolve. He pulled back and looked at the flush of her cheeks and her swollen tender lips. His kiss was still on her.

"Good night, Hana," he said longingly, then stood, raised her hand and brushed his lips over her the back of her fingers before he left.

Chapter Twenty-Three

Adrian was coiled tight. His body yearned for Hana's, and his heart was experiencing severe emotional turbulence. He couldn't process all that at the moment. His sister was chauffeuring him to lunch with their mother in her car, a Firecracker red Jeep Rubicon with the top off. The wind was blowing both his and her hair into a frenzy of whipped chaos.

Adrian turned his eyes to watch the road. He regretted accepting her offer to collect him.

"You're going too fast," he told her angry at her recklessness. All the other cars seemed to be going much slower than they were, and she had to make frequent lane changes to maintain her speed. It was dangerous.

As Lisa went up a gear to catch a yellow light, he glanced at her and scowled. She ignored him, her bright blonde hair flying around her head. She was wearing a pinstripe royal blue suit with a black button-down shirt and had paired the ensemble with red lipstick, which matched the paint of her car.

Damn. Her blue blazer was identical to his and so were their coordinating suit pants. Even the striped pattern of the fabric looked the same. Adrian thought they looked ridiculous.

She glanced at him briefly. "I'm going only fifteen over the limit." She grinned. "You always told me speeding would be twenty."

"I taught you how to drive ten over," Adrian said sharply. "Good thing we're in your car, not mine." He heard at least three cars honking as she switched lanes into the far right on the incline of a hill.

"You can't cross here," he yelled. "Lisa!"

Adrian grabbed the grab handle above his head and held on as she made a sharp right turn. She had one hand on the armrest as she braked to hug the curve of the road. He feared he'd die in this Jeep, which was far from his life plan.

"I'm an excellent driver," Lisa declared. "I got us here ten minutes earlier than expected." She tilted her chin in the direction of the restaurant.

"I'm not hungry anymore," he muttered.

"Why? Because of Hana?"

"Because of your driving," Adrian snapped. "Pay attention to the road." Lisa turned back to face forward in time to brake at a stop sign.

She said, "You could tell her the truth."

Adrian rolled his eyes. "I'm getting nauseous from this car ride."

"You're in love with her, and for whatever idiotic reason you've come up with, you haven't told her yet." She kept going. "I adore watching you in love. You look terrified."

Adrian shook his head and admitted, "She doesn't love me."

"I saw how she looked at you," Lisa told him. "Though I think she could do better, she seemed to be into you."

"I don't want to talk about this."

Lisa grunted, and he gave her a bit more of his truth. "If Hana doesn't love me, it's because I made it difficult for her to do so."

Lisa slowed down as she gave him a sidelong glance. "Have you apologized to her for whatever you did? I mean, properly?"

He shrugged. "I want to change the subject."

"She might surprise you," Lisa said ignoring his wishes.

"Thank you for playing the optimist, but save it for mom." He looked down and sent Hana a message. It would probably be days before she got back to him. He'd be like Pumpkin, waiting for her to decide to return to him.

***

Hana got a text from Adrian asking if she was available for dinner. She smiled, maybe one day she could convince him to cook instead of going out. She'd teach him a couple of things in the kitchen, like how to work an oven, a stand mixer, and a sauté pan. He would probably teach her some things too. Indecent things she'd come to crave.

She texted him she was available and wondered what the night would hold. Later, standing in front of her closet, she chose one of her best dresses, and had tamed her curls into submission in a high ponytail. She had put on her FM shoes and wore her thigh highs. She felt invincible.

Earlier than they'd planned, she walked into Adrian's office tower, took the elevator up to his floor and made her way over to Louis the second, as she'd dubbed him in her head. She held her hand up when he picked up the phone. She wanted to surprise Adrian, but first, she had to know. "Is your real name Louis?"

He looked up at her. He couldn't be more than twenty-five. Cute in a suit, and excessively muscled. Not like the other Louis at all. This was the imposter Louis.

"Yes, of course," he answered in an annoyed tone. He was looking at her like she was crazy.

"Have you ever met the other Louis?" she asked.

"I—" He stopped and sighed loudly. The original Louis was definitely more polite. "Do you want me to tell Mr. Douglas you're here or not?"

Who did Adrian hire first, she wondered, gentleman Louis or pretty boy Louis? She couldn't help but worry that Adrian had only hired him because his name was also Louis. It couldn't be because of this young man's sparkling personality. He was quite rude.

She shook her head. "I'll tell him. Thanks." Louis rolled his eyes.

She walked up to the door of Adrian's office and opened it to find him where he probably spent eighty percent of his life. At his desk. His fingers were tented in front of him as he seemed to watch her walk into the room. He didn't look like himself. He looked disheveled.

Normally smoothed down, his hair was standing up in odd places, his skin looked wind burned, and his cheeks were reddened. His bright blue suit blazer was on a valet stand in the corner, and his tie wasn't around his neck. As if all of that wasn't shocking, he'd unbuttoned a couple of the top buttons on his shirt.

He had a dazed look on his face, which he blinked away making her think he hadn't really seen her come in at all.

"I have something I want to talk to you about," she announced.

***

Oh god. It was happening. Hana was going to break the contract. The deception, the lies, and the manipulation had all come crashing down, and now he was going to lose the only woman he had ever loved. She'd let herself in wearing those gladiator heels, ready to stomp all over his black heart. His eyes traveled the length of her, wanting to lick his lips at that dress which tightly clung to her devastating curves.

The deep vee hinted at her abundant cleavage. Damn. She was on fire and clearly dressed for battle. He was helpless. He'd probably sign over his company if she asked.

He attempted to stop the inevitable and asked, "Ready for dinner?" He looked into her rich brown eyes and prayed he could have one more chance with his angel. One more night.

"Now?" He'd distracted her from what she was going to say. She walked closer and sat down in the chair in front of his desk, and slowly crossed her legs.

His mouth went dry and he had to swallow twice to answer. "Yes. Right now."

"Fine." She agreed too easily. She had a piece of paper in her hand and she fingered the edge of it. She was calm and cool, like she had all the time in the world. She said. "I want to talk about something first. Business first, then pleasure."

"I want to take you on a trip," he blurted out. He'd never felt so nervous before. He adjusted the shoulders of his shirt over his arms. The fabric felt tight across his chest.

"A trip," she repeated with a skeptical laugh.

"To Rome." He threw out Italy. Then, "Or Japan."

He realized how idiotic he sounded. She had to be silently laughing at him.

She continued rubbing the two halves of a mysterious note together without responding. He realized he had a slight tremor to his voice and tried to clear his throat. She had to see how nervous he was.

"Wherever you want to go," he offered. Adrian gave up and shut his mouth. He didn't want to say the words *I love you* out loud, deciding to communicate with his eyes.

Hana tilted her head. He liked the way she had pinned back the curls from her face on one side. He liked everything about her. The brown eyes, the smiling lips. Though, she wasn't smiling now. "Not today, Adrian."

"Next week," he said offered, trying to bargain with her.

She shook her head at him. "I'm not flying away with you."

"You have to," he insisted. He couldn't lose her. Not yet. In his convoluted way, he was telling her he was in love with her. He was wearing his heart on his sleeve. He had nothing left to lose by not saying it. If she was going to leave at least she would know how he felt.

"Is it in my contract?" She raised a brow.

That cursed agreement. Adrian was on a direct and fiery path to rejection, and Hana was turning icy. He could say anything he wanted to. For some absurd reason, she'd never read the damn thing. Adrian couldn't lie to her, He shook his head.

"Then I'll go," she said, smiling. It was like the sun came out after three weeks of rain. "I want to give you something first."

She put her hand out to give him the paper. He had to keep his hand from trembling as he reached across the desk.

"This is my first check," she declared.

"Check?" He unfolded the small slip. It was a check for ten thousand dollars.

"It's my first payment to you."

He didn't understand, he looked at the check, then back at her.

"I'm going to have to do it in installments." She shrugged. "I hope the amounts will increase and I'll pay you back in full as soon as I can."

"You don't owe me anything." She got out of the chair and walked around his desk to stand before him. He took her hands in his. "I'm sorry I brought money into this." He stood. "Can we ever forget about it?"

"No," she said firmly. "We can't."

She leaned her face up and kissed him. The touch was whisper soft against his lips and it soothed his aching heart. She put a hand on his hard chest, and he felt it in his bones.

"You see I have a plan." She looked him straight in the eye. "I took my million-dollar salary and donated it to Esperanza. From the other nine million, I took five hundred thousand to—"

He cut her off with a kiss. Then whispered, "I love you, Hana." The words were in the air, and he couldn't take them back. He didn't want to. He didn't dare move or breathe while he waited for her response. She made him suffer. There was a long pregnant pause as she considered him, looking up into his eyes as if to see if he was telling the truth.

She smiled and seeing it recalibrated the beat of his heart. She pulled back and said, "I've always wanted to go to Edinburgh." She put her hands on his face, framing it and said the words he needed to hear. "I want to go with you."

Chapter Twenty-Four

The feeling of Hana's hand in his had him soaring higher than the Gulfstream he'd hired to take them to Edinburgh. After they took off, she settled in next to him and put her head on his shoulder. Adrian kissed her forehead. He never knew he could feel like this. Only Hana could to this to him.

Though... she hadn't told him she loved him. She hadn't even responded to his declaration, but he comforted himself with the fact that she was here. That had to mean she was all in, didn't it? Actions spoke louder than words. Hana may not love him now, but she might one day. He'd wait. As long as she was with him, he'd wait an eternity for her love.

Between getting the check and now, he'd learned she and Taron had started a business with the sole intent of using the profits to fund Esperanza. They'd set up a website and had partnered with a few outlets that carried products made by people in emerging countries. But the money hadn't come from there. It was interest on the nine million dollars she hadn't used, but had invested, and kept enough cash liquid to start paying him back. She meant to give him all ten million as soon as she could.

He tried not to care she hadn't told him about T+H until today. Hana had secrets. She didn't want to share everything she was planning with him yet, and he couldn't expect her to. He would have to earn her trust. He loved the idea of her new business, but he wondered why she hadn't wanted to tell him about it until now.

He'd never tell her he wasn't going to cash any of the checks she gave him. He didn't want her money, he wanted her. If she didn't want his money, then how else would he convince her to stay with him? He didn't have any redeemable qualities, and, according to her, had no moral compass. He hated this foreign feeling of being helpless. He couldn't sleep for all the roiling in his brain.

They landed in Gatwick to refuel and were scheduled to land in Edinburgh at sunset. His favorite time of day. He pulled up the window shutter and the golden rays cascaded over him. He turned to look at Hana who was still asleep, the sunset illuminating her face. He gazed upon that visage which had become so beloved to him and sighed.

He couldn't fathom an existence where he couldn't look at her. He could see every freckle on her nose and the soft tawny gold of her skin. He watched the soft rustle of her eyelids and memorized every line of her features. She was still leaning on his shoulder, and the touch was comforting and familiar. He could sit here for an eternity and watch her snore angelically.

Her dark curls softly framed her face. He couldn't dream up a more exquisite sublimity, but he had never feared losing her more. Even though she was with him, he remained vigilant for signs she'd leave him at any time. He was that irredeemable. She hadn't even seen what he had brought with him to Edinburgh.

***

Hana opened her eyes and peered up at Adrian. She wondered how long he'd been staring at her. Except for the first couple of hours after they took off, when he told her about Lisa's driving, their lunch with their mother, and other inconsequential but personal, getting to know you things, Hana slept.

She blinked a couple times to clear her eyes, Adrian had been reading on his iPad. She'd never seen him read a book before. She liked that about him. He was a secret reader. There were many things she'd like to know about him. The next thing would be to know exactly what he was thinking while he stared at her.

She smiled at him.

"This my favorite time of day," he told her. She knew that about him. Adrian loved sunsets.

She lifted her head. "You know, you can't buy a sunset, Mr. Douglas, so don't try."

"I know that." He mused and looked out the window. "Even I know that." He glanced out the window. "There are some things in the world that are so beautiful no one could buy them."

Hana didn't say anything. She understood the subtext. He regretted the contract. She appreciated knowing that. Adrian was changing, she could see the transformation written all over his perfect face. Hana kissed his chiseled cheek and grabbed his hand in hers. He squeezed back gently. Her hand felt protected in his.

He brushed the hair back from her face with his free hand and looked into her eyes. "Beautiful. Absolutely beautiful." He wasn't talking about the sunset anymore.

***

He pressed his lips to hers at the same time the plane hit the tarmac. The kiss burned his lips, the touch of her soft perfect mouth pressing into his. Adrian would love Hana until the day he died, and he hoped his kiss told her all the things he couldn't say. The entire plane shook as they locked lips. She gripped Adrian's hand and it was his turn to pull back and smile.

The plane turned into their gate. Hana unbuckled her seatbelt and stood up. Adrian grabbed their bags and led the way off the plane. He had a car arranged to take them down the royal mile near Edinburgh castle where they'd be staying in a private suite in a turret. She said nothing as they climbed the curved stairway to arrive at their suite of rooms with a spectacular view of the city from Old Town rooftops to Princes Street, and over the Firth of Forth to Fife and beyond.

She fell silent as she walked into the sitting room paneled in lacquer red leather that was larger than her whole apartment. Adrian tipped the bellman then shut the door behind them.

Hana murmured that she had to use the bathroom then disappeared. A few minutes later she came out completely soaked. She stood at the doorway and looked at him raining water onto the carpet. Her hair was a wet blanket over her shoulders and the water was dripping onto the tops of the globes of her amber breasts. The rest of her body was gently covered by a fluffy white bath towel. Steam poured from the bathroom, and the flush of warmth was visible on the tops of her collarbones and on her cheeks. Desire coursed through him making him weak in the knees.

He loosened his tie and made his intentions known. He wasn't going to let Hana leave this room until he had made her his.

He walked over to her and sank to his knees, and looked up at her sweet face, waiting for her approval, her permission. There were no contracts. Only a man on his knees praying for a second chance, Adrian reached up and grabbed a fistful of the towel and waited.

***

Hana was holding onto her towel by the top edge. She felt the heady sensation of need overtaking her. His eyes promised wicked pleasure if only she'd consent. He was asking her to risk her heart and meet him in the fire of their passion. He could burn her heart to the ground with the sweep of those green eyes over her body.

Adrian had stripped off his blazer and tie and was at her feet kneeling like a fallen angel waiting for her to say yes. Hana bit her lip and nodded. Adrian wetted his lips with his tongue sinfully and smiled, and she felt it right between her legs as she let him take the towel from her body.

He had come to claim her.

Hana stood before Adrian like Aphrodite. Her breasts were bare and the tips pebbled under the cool air and his appraisal. She felt so wantonly exposed under his gaze. His eyes danced as he swept his gaze over her body.

He was so close if she lifted her leg, he could put his mouth on her. The thought alone made her wet. Adrian put his hand up and touched her belly. The touch was surprising in its intimacy. His hand squeezed gently on her abdomen and then traveled on a path to her thigh. The sensation of his touch drew all the blood to her aching sex.

He waited patiently for her signal she was ready. She put both hands around his chiseled face, holding the storm of her man's emotions in her hands.

She couldn't control the sea, the sky, or the tempest of him, and she didn't want to. She wanted to release his obsession on her.

Hana craved his touch, and she missed his hands on her body. She wouldn't deny herself again.

She bent down and touched her lips to his gently. She loved Adrian more than he would ever know. He responded by picking her up and wrapping her legs around his waist. He carried her like a prize to the bed, and she wondered if he was the villain or the hero of her story.

Chapter Twenty-Five

Adrian bent down to kiss Hana as she fell onto the bed. He savored the taste of her lips: sugary sweet with tender surrender. He felt the need in her kiss as she propped herself up on her elbows. He wanted to make out with her languidly. She wanted him to make love to her quickly, but he refused. He would deepen the layers of the seduction by placing them at a leisurely pace. He intended to savor Hana like the delicacy she was.

Adrian pushed his tongue into her mouth and stroked hers deeply. She put her arms around his neck and held on. He took everything she offered, pressing his body into hers. He moved his knee between her naked thighs his leg still covered by his pants. He tried to unbutton his shirt, but Hana pulled the shirt over his head impatiently.

His pulse quickened as he chased a fiery path of pleasure down the column of her neck. Now that she had acquiesced, Adrian had a mind to mark every part of her body as his. He worshipped the crook of her neck with pulls of his mouth and teeth, and then suckled on the skin above her breasts. He moved his head down to pull her nipple into his mouth. He worshipped the puckering tip by suckling so hard she gasped. He released her breast to the air then followed it with a punishing lap of his tongue. He intended to have her writhing beneath him, begging for release.

Adrian tortured her by continuously pulling the flesh of her nipple in his mouth and sucking on it then releasing it into the cold air. He wanted her to feel it in her toes. He moved to her stomach, dragging his teeth on the soft skin. She grabbed the crown of his head to either stop him or make him go lower. He looked up at her wanting to know which.

Hana's eyes glowed and her breasts were squeezed through the funnel of her arms.

Adrian had never been more turned on his life. His hardened cock throbbed begging to be inside of her. He'd stop if she asked, though it might kill him. He kissed the rise of her stomach and patiently waited for her to let him continue. He had all the time in the world to spend on her. When she gave him a small smile of approval, he had to keep his control in check. He wanted to devour her. Ravish her. Instead he took in the look in her eyes: slightly dazed and pleasure glazed. He loved having an effect on her. He planned on keeping her like this for hours each day and night.

Hana bit her lip again and the sight of it had him putting his palm on her lower stomach, close to juncture of her thighs. He held her gaze and dared her to continue to watch him. She didn't blink as he took his hand and trailed it down from her navel and touched her core. She dropped her head back and surrendered.

Adrian chuckled shamelessly and pulled her thighs apart. His need to taste her nearly overwhelmed him. He put his lips to one thigh and gently nipped at it, then nuzzled.

***

Hana dropped her head to the bed after seeing all the things Adrian intended to do to her in his eyes. It was too much. She caught her breath and felt his lips graze her throbbing sex. He took her into his mouth like he did every other part of her body, greedily. He used his tongue to create a suction against her that was so sinful she screamed.

Adrian lapped at her with depraved attention. She felt the waves of pleasure building as she ascended to new heights. He continued with his carnal kisses against her sex. The tension of what was going to be an unbelievable climax had her pulling on his hair to put his face deeper into her sex. Her hips bucked and he held onto her hips, keeping his mouth on her.

Masterfully, Adrian was orchestrating the most mind-blowing orgasm of her life. He pulled at the lips of her labia with his teeth, and then sucked on her clit to draw out the pleasure. Hana shattered and screamed his name as Adrian held her thighs down and continued to lap at her. It was too much, and not nearly enough.

Urgently, she jackknifed up and helped him remove his pants, but not before he grabbed a condom from the pocket and rolled it on.

***

Hana pulled Adrian into a kiss and had to have tasted herself on his lips. He was so turned on the stiffness was painful. She wrapped her legs around his waist, reached down and grabbed him. The touch was white hot as she led him to her entrance. She was so wet, he slid right in.

He was unmanned by the pleasure of sliding into her hot sheath. Hana tugged at his lips with her teeth, demanding another orgasm. He was dedicated to giving it to her.

He pressed forward until he was completely inside of her, and felt the spasm of her muscles until he could go no farther. She gasped and tightened her legs around his waist. This was where he was always meant to be. It felt like home. He pulled out and the absence of her heat had him thrusting back in desperately.

He pumped quickly and impatiently, drunk on the feeling of returning back to the comfort of her. She was his woman and no one else's. He took command of her lips and then his hand met the place between their bodies, found her clit and squeezed. Adrian wanted to ensure she was riding that wave with him.

Adrian tweaked and rubbed with his fingers, and with his mouth, he captured every moan and gasp coming up Hana's throat. He would never get enough of her, and he intended to spend a lifetime attempting to.

The telling pulsation of her inner muscles told Adrian her orgasm was upon her. He thrust one more time, filling her and stilling inside of her. They clasped each other with heaving chests until Adrian collapsed with heavenly exhaustion.

***

Hana caught her breath and looked at Adrian wondering if the passion would always be this strong between them. It was startling how much he could make her feel when he kissed her. Hana knew she was ruined for other men.

Hana knew it would take time for him to learn how to be warm and generous, and for them to heal from the way they began. It was easy to make hasty decisions when the fire burned so brightly, and to make declarations of everlasting love when his kisses felt so right.

They'd never gone away together, and Hana wanted it to be a great memory they'd have together forever.

Their attraction had taken center stage when friendship should have been the star. She planned to have that friendship now, and relish when the passion overcame them. No doubt, Adrian had seduced her body. Hana planned to seduce his heart. She didn't trust his admission of love. Love was time, trust, and patience. She didn't believe love couldn't be true when it was only five months old and built on a guilt-ridden foundation.

She could see it in his puppy dog-eyed moments of vulnerability that he wanted her to tell him she loved him too. He was eager to be in love with her, but he'd never even been in a relationship before. She needed time to trust he meant what he said and was going to stick.

Hana would make him take baby steps, and when she was ready to run, she'd tell him.

They curled into each other and before she drifted off to sleep, Adrian said, "Good night, my love."

The next morning, he woke her with his mouth between her legs. As alarm clocks went, it was perfect. After they'd enjoyed each other completely, she sat up and moved off the bed, pulling her clothes out of the bag.

"Get ready, Mr. Douglas, we're leaving this suite."

Adrian gave her a lazy morning smile, and the sight of it made her heart twist. It would be a long and difficult wait to proper romance, to true love, but he looked like he was worth the wait. She watched him distractedly while he jogged his naked behind to the bathroom and came out thirty minutes later impeccably dressed in another pressed suit.

Hana laughed. He was a handsome devil, she'd admit. He was going to try to beguile her every chance he got. She saw it in his sparkling green eyes.

They walked hand in hand to the elevator. It was the first time they had ever done that– held hands in public. She felt like a teenager, giddy and delirious. It was ludicrous to be so happy with a man who she was just beginning to trust. She looked at her reflection in the elevator mirror. She looked wild.

Hana did her best to smooth down her hair while Adrian snickered and fought to hold her hand again. Hana brushed his hand away and batted at her head. Her hair was fatally frizzed and her curls were haphazard after being dried by rolling around on bed sheets. It was the worst possible way to style hair, making love with Adrian. He smiled at her shyly and let her lead him out to the street. He probably felt vulnerable without the two Louises.

She let the charm of Scotland seep into her bones and took them to the nearest pub under Adrian's protest. He preferred to frequent restaurants where he'd booked a reservation. She wanted local color. They ate hearty soup and Adrian managed to look as ridiculous with a napkin stuffed in his suit as he had back home. She wanted to see as many sights as they could see, and he was complaining about the quality of the dinner linen.

She kissed him after she threw some money down on the table.

"I hope you're ready, Adrian."

Chapter Twenty-Six

Hana made him walk through the streets, and it was so cold he bought them lined gloves at a corner store, of all things. She was in love with Edinburgh, of course. She loved the elegant old gray bricks and the colorful row houses in Old Town near the pub. It reminded her of San Francisco, then she said it was like no other place in the world. He was glad to be with her, he wanted to propose to her every time she laughed while they were walking.

He had never been so smitten in his life. He was ready to drop to a knee every time she hugged his arm and thanked him for taking her there.

Her joy at being in Edinburgh only enhanced her beauty. Her dark curls streamed down her back, and her eyes were glowing. Everything charmed her, and she was sweet when she looked up at him to confirm he thought the city was wonderful too. Seeing her like this, he vowed to take her on a vacation every time she was able to tear herself away from work.

They walked up and down the royal mile and strolled through the manicured Princess Gardens.

He wished he had Louis to drive him, but he wouldn't accept the comfort if it meant missing the wind whipping Hana's hair like a tornado around her face. She fought the invisible foe and Adrian broke out in full unrestrained laughter as the wind blew her hair into a frenzy.

The wind made a fool out of his suits too and the blazer tips had wings flying around his waist. He was inappropriately dressed and Hana was getting the most joy at mocking him. They bundled up and continued the hike up Edinburgh Castle. When they reached the climbable peak, he hugged her for warmth near the edge of the precipice overlooking the city.

He had a thought, an inspiration standing there. He shivered and held out his hand, he had all the time in the world to freeze on the top of this castle waiting for Hana to dance with him. She laughed so hard, she wheezed. Adrian wanted to make her laugh for the rest of his life and dance with her all the time.

"Adrian," she exclaimed as if she was going to say no. "We are going to freeze to death."

"Before we do, I want to dance." He was a fool in love.

She smiled and took his hand. "I would be crazy to accept."

He inclined his head in agreement and then folded her into his arms and turned them into a slow dance. Hana put her arms around his neck. She was shivering as he put his other arm around her waist. The music in his head floated over them. He knew she could hear it in the beat of his heart as he looked into her eyes.

Adrian hoped this was enough for her to see how much he truly loved her. He was going to buy her flowers and dance with her as often as he dared. She deserved that and more. Every word of a sonnet and flattering poetry he could learn. He would learn, he vowed sweeping her across the invisible dance floor.

***

So much for her resolve. Hana gazed up at Adrian and thought, *he's truly my prince*. She'd probably develop hypothermia in a couple of minutes, but it was worth it to be in his arms as he danced her around a castle. This was the romantic feeling she'd never dreamed of having. She was a California girl in a billionaire's arms, and wondered if this was love, real love, and that she wasn't going to be able to shake him for the rest of her life.

Hana laughed and hugged his side. She was really cold. She looked over the edge of the stone wall at the city. "Now there's a view I'd like to see out my window."

Adrian murmured his agreement and put his arm over her shoulder, and it helped. She was still in awe. He had told her he loved her, and though it was hard to believe, she took a leap of faith. He might really love her.

He seemed to know a little of the history of the area. He pointed to Arthur's Seat. "That was a volcano," he commented, hugging her tightly.

She wondered if he had been here before. She promised she'd find out everything about him before she married him. That thought nearly knocked her off her feet, yet it seemed to feel right. Inevitable.

"Can we climb it?" she asked. She hoped her enthusiasm would be enough to convince him. She hoped to convince him to do everything on this trip: let his hair down, take his pretty boy suit off and wear boots so they could trek in the mud.

He shook his head. "Of course, you'd want to climb a mountain. I thought we'd find a nice restaurant instead." Adrian laughed. "But I'll do it if you ask."

"Well, I'm asking."

She had hope for him yet. Hana grabbed his hand and they marched out toward the other peak, descending the castle hill.

"I really wish I had Louis right now," Adrian huffed. Hana patted his arm. He really was ridiculous. They got closer to the base of Arthur's Seat, and began the hike up the mountain huffing and stopping. They were out of breath.

"You're so spoiled."

He looked affronted, but said, "You're the only person I've met who works harder than I do. Starting a new business to feed your charity. You're one of the few people I know who could pull it off."

Well, that was nice. She shrugged. "Necessity is the mother of invention."

"You know," he said between gasps for breath, "I would've become an early investor if you let me."

"Absolutely not," she shouted. "You and I are never making another contract again."

He shook his head. "Isn't that what marriage is, a contract?" In a way he was right, but in the most important way, he was wrong. "You would never consider engaging in another contract with me?" he asked softly. He made marriage sound so binding, so controlling. Adrian's issues came to the fore.

"Marriage is a union between two people, the contract is incidental. The partnership is fundamental. There isn't money involved in that kind of relationship."

He shrugged. "But I can provide money when you need it. You'll have an annual stipend ranging in the millions and increasing every year we're together."

Hana thought he made the whole thing sound so business-like. Marriage was about love. For Hana it had to be about love. She didn't care what other women needed, she had to have Adrian's love, not his money. She didn't judge how any woman put food on her table, but she didn't think of marriage as a financial arrangement. She was uncomfortable enough that he was wealthy in the first place. His house and his parents' home freaked her out like when Elizabeth Darcy walked through Pemberley.

Sometimes he got the right of it when he was all tea, flowers, and castle dancing, but then he said stuff like, "I can give you an annual stipend ranging in the millions and increasing every year we're together," she wanted to punch him,

"You wrote up a contract," she guessed.

"I have it with me," he confirmed, patting his blazer.

"I'm working on getting rid of the last one," she yelled. People passed around them, looking at her like she was off her mind. She pulled Adrian to the side so they could argue alone on a small peak on Arthur's Seat. "Is this some sort of proposal Adrian?" Hana hissed. "Because if it is, it's terrible."

She focused on the bright yellow wildflowers under her feet, and Adrian led her further towards a solitary spot near a precipice. The view of the entire city of Edinburgh was below them, and the first rays of a sunset were visible.

Adrian frowned. "Why is it terrible? I want to marry you. I know it's not a financially sound move, but I'm trying to put a price on the happiness you've brought to me. It's made my life so much better."

This was the worst proposal she'd ever heard. "I can't believe you think that's a marriage proposal. It's almost worse than your first offer."

He scoffed and folded his arms. They both were wordless holding their frigid chests and gazing at each other. She hated everything he was saying.

"Why do you think you have to buy my love?" Hana asked him softly. "You think that money is the only way I'll be with you?" She put a hand up to his face. "I have all the money I need." She kissed him softly and pulled back. "I'm not going to marry you Adrian. If this is your proposal today then I'm saying no."

Adrian was shocked. "You don't want to marry me?" He looked at her defiantly.

***

There it was. Hana would never marry him.

He pulled out the contract and put it in her hands. He put his heart in her hands. She took it and looked down at the stack of paper in her fingers. It provided for anything she could want, money to care for herself and their family with no stipulations on how she wanted to spend it. The contract was his declaration of intent, power over everything he owned, his love included.

"One day when you ask me without a contract in your hand, I'll say yes," she stated harshly. "You can't buy me."

She ripped up the contract and it felt like she was stomping on his heart. He didn't know how to propose properly. He didn't know if she ever wanted to hear another proposal from him. She didn't look at him, and he knew he had made another horrible mistake.

Hana turned to him and said, "I'm in love with you." His heart soared. "There's no price for that. You're breaking my heart, and there's no way to repair that. There's not enough money in the world."

Adrian dropped to his knees, ruining his suit in the Scottish mud. He didn't want to let her go. He'd learn how to say it correctly.

"Marry me without the contract," he begged. "Marry me because I love you. Marry me because I'll spend the rest of my life loving you." He grabbed her hands.

"Keep your money, and give me your heart," she said as if she hadn't heard his heartfelt declaration. "I'm worth it."

"You already have it. You always have." He stood up, and in front of the mountain and everyone in Edinburgh, he took her face in his hands and kissed her.

Hana pulled back from his kiss. "I won't marry anyone I've known for half a day."

He dove back in and kissed her into silence. He was looking forward to spending the rest of his life kissing this woman into silence. He was a damn fool, but he wouldn't change one thing about her.

When he'd taken her breath away, he pulled back and stated, "Half a year. We've known each other half a year."

"Our love will deepen in time. When I'm ready I'll know it." She said looking into his eyes. "We'll both know it."

"I already know it." He swore he'd marry her today if he could. He was going to need to be resuscitated if he kept throwing his heart at her. "I want you forever."

She shook her head. "In a year say that to me and I'll believe it."

"Half a year," he told her. Hana loved him, and that's all he needed to know.

"Now you're negotiating." She laughed. She kissed him soundly. "Seven months."

"Some of that must include the engagement," Adrian said, condensing how long it would take to make her his wife.

"The engagement is a waiting process, Mr. Douglas."

She captured his lips and talked bureaucracy against his helpless kiss. "There are licenses and waiting periods. Why, you'll have to draw up another contract."

Adrian growled and captured her lips, nibbling on her bottom one. They'd need to get back to the suite.

"I insist upon an elopement," he stated.

Hana pulled back and put his hand in hers. She led him to the path to walk him down from the peak. She laughed. "Not in ten million years."

"Twelve months from the day we met for the engagement and wedding," he demanded, grabbing her hand and pulling her to his side.

"Deal."

Adrian's heart dropped into his stomach, bounced around for a moment, then soared through his body like a shot of light. He stopped and hugged so tight he could feel her ribs through her clothes, Added bonus, he was covering her in mud too.

Adrian set her down and put his hand out for her. "Deal, Ms. Romero Douglas."

She shook her head and put her hand out. He took her hand to his lips and kissed the knuckles like he did that first night at the gala.

She considered him, her eyes softening. "Maybe shorten the engagement. I've reconsidered the terms."

"What about right now?"

"Too soon, Mr. Douglas." She took his arm and they walked down the hill.

"I prefer you immediately in all circumstances, Ms. Romero Douglas."

"Who am I to deny you then?" she said softly. He drew her back into the circle of his arms and kissed her.

"Is it soon to move in?" he asked knowing her answer.

"Come on Mr. Douglas, you know it is."

He shook his head and bent down, kissing her senseless until she changed her mind.

ABOUT THE AUTHOR

Giselle is an author of contemporary love stories where she focuses on empowering women and challenging the damsel in distress narrative. She's performed in poetry readings, written tons of stories, and read hundreds of romance novels. Her day job: she's a licensed medical professional who proudly serves Veterans.

Connect with Giselle:
website: gisellewatersromance.com
IG: @gisellewatersromance
FB: /giselle.waters.1485
twitter: @GiselleWaters6

www.BOROUGHSPUBLISHINGGROUP.com

If you enjoyed this book, please write a review. Our authors appreciate the feedback, and it helps future readers find books they love. We welcome your comments and invite you to send them to info@boroughspublishinggroup.com. Follow us on Facebook, Twitter and Instagram, and be sure to sign up for our newsletter for surprises and new releases from your favorite authors.

Are you an aspiring writer? Check out www.boroughspublishinggroup.com/submit and see if we can help you make your dreams come true.

www.ingramcontent.com/pod-product-compliance
Lightning Source LLC
Chambersburg PA
CBHW071346170626
46811CB00003B/1007

* 9 7 8 1 9 5 3 8 1 0 3 5 9 *